PRAISE FOR BIRD BY KIM E. WILSON

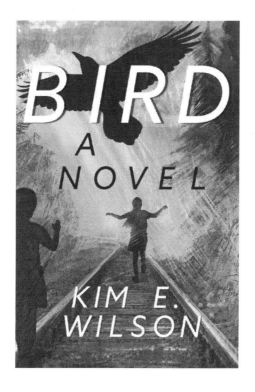

"I love stories that piece the story together using flashbacks. Bird does this and does it well. Tiny, seemingly inconsequential clues from the flashbacks move the story along quickly leaving the reader feeling like they are discovering two stories."

"This book grabbed me from the very beginning! "

"LOVED the book! Great visual descriptions... felt immersed in the story during it's entirety.... both physically and emotionally. "

"I really liked the story with the flip flopping timelines."

"Very sweet book. "

"A must-read for the summer."

The Fireflies of Estill County

Kim E. Wilson

kimewilson.com

BISAC Categories:

FIC074000 **FICTION** / Southern

FIC022070 **FICTION** / Mystery & Detective / Cozy

Summary:

Bertie Dunnigan, a seasoned criminal defense attorney living in Louisville, receives an anonymous email with the subject heading "Fireflies." She knows even before opening it that the worst night of her life has come back to haunt her. Now she must revisit her childhood in Kentucky in order to understand her past.

ISBN: 9798675695096

 EmeraldPublishers

DEDICATION

For the fireflies in my life: Sharon, Lisa, Jody, Melissa, Shawna, Carol, Abby, Kristina, Katy, and in loving memory of Jane.

*"I slept under the moonlight and set my soul free,
caged within jars like fireflies."*

-Prajakta Mhadnak

PROLOGUE

The email subject reads "Fireflies." I stare at it. My heart races, bile rises in my throat, my palms are sweating, my mouth is dry, I'm paralyzed. I blink. I blink again. It's still there. *Go away! You're not there, are you? Open it! No! Do it! No! Delete it! NO!!! Why not? Because you can't, can you?* Because I can't. My fingers tremble as I click on it. There are only three simple words: "Can we meet?" I silently scream. *No. No. No. No!* I can't do that. We can't do that! I shove my fist in my mouth, my teeth sinking into my own flesh. I rock back and forth to stop the panic rising within me. Why now? Why after all these years? We made a solemn promise to each other: no contact unless we were in real trouble. Oh God! That's it. One of them is in trouble, or maybe one of them is about to betray the rest of us. No, they wouldn't do that. We would never betray each other. I don't have a choice. I made that promise too. I reach out, hit reply, and type "when and where?" I stare at my words, then hit send. Now I wait.

Present Day

ONE

"Brrr...April, you suck!" I say, pulling up the collar of my trench coat and tightening the belt around my waist. Springtime in Louisville is a crap shoot. There's that one day, that one glorious day, when the promise of spring bursts forth, then *whoosh*, the tickle of that warm day and early morning birdsong vanishes, carried away on the remaining winter winds. That glorious day was yesterday: sunny, high sixties, the smell of spring in the air. The weather was spectacular. It's what we locals call Derby weather, the kind this town hopes for in the weeks leading up to the fastest two minutes in sports, the Kentucky Derby. Yesterday was so beautiful that I even went jogging in Cherokee Park. Today, Mother Nature has turned manic. I can even see my breath. It must have plummeted nearly thirty degrees since last night. I'm running a bit later than usual. I don't normally sleep past seven a.m., but the chill in the house kept me under the covers. Besides, the jury may or may not reach a verdict by the end of the week. My client, Emma Davies, has been waiting for three days to learn her fate. It's excruciating. Believe me, I know the toll waiting can take on a person. It's been over a week since I received that email. So far nothing. That email's been taking up real estate in my brain and has made it difficult—no, damn near impossible—for me to give my full attention to the trial. It's not fair to Emma that my mind's been elsewhere, but I think my closing arguments were good regardless. We'll see soon enough how effective I was with this jury. And yet, how can I be anything but distracted? I don't want to lose the life I've worked so hard for.

Despite the cold temperatures, the birds are singing. It's amazing. I feel like everything's on the verge of falling apart, and yet, the damn birds are still singing. I breathe in the cold air as I hop into the car and start the engine, adjusting the heat to maximum. Cold air blasts me. My little Subaru, which I lovingly refer to as Lil' piece of shit, takes her time waking up. She's a lot like me. I really should think about getting another car, but I know I won't anytime soon. I grip the frigid steering wheel, wishing I'd remembered my gloves, but they're still stuffed in the pocket of my winter coat that's hanging in the closet. I wish I'd worn my boots instead of these three-inch Sam Edelman heels. Also, slacks would have been a better choice than my don't-I-look-sophisticated charcoal-gray pencil skirt. I'm not sure why I selected this outfit today. Normally, I'm more practical in my fashion selections. The older I'm getting the less I care about outer appearances, but this case is too high profile and many eyes are on us. Besides, I don't have time to go back and change my clothes or retrieve my gloves or boots. My head feels cloudy, and I'm so cold my tits are standing at attention. I just need to get into the office and get coffee, a lot of coffee. My pocket vibrates. *Noooo...please, nooo...*I just need an hour. I feel sick. My world feels shaky. I fish the phone out of my coat pocket and see that it's Beaker. Here we go...

"Hey, what's going on, Beaker?" I ask my law clerk with fear in my voice.

"Hey Bertie, where are you?" he asks.

"Just left my house. What's happening?"

"The jury's in. Get here ASAP!" Beaker bestowed himself with that name because of his prominent nose. He's got a really kind face, but the lengthy nose and scraggily goatee make him look more like a beatnik from the 1960s. He's a gifted law clerk, a bit different though. Aren't the good ones always a bit different? He's never mentioned a girlfriend since he's been with the firm, but I've caught him gazing at my daughter Annie. I believe he has deep feelings for her, I can see it in his eyes. She adores him too, but only as a friend, maybe even more like a brother. Still, regardless of the relationship, they work fantastically well together. Beaker's heavily into video games and loves to play the card game Magic, both online and in tournaments. He spends his evenings at various music shows around town and can tell you the name of any band playing locally on any given night. Annie's extremely athletic, plays tennis, and loves watching soccer. She's charismatic and self-assured, both great assets for a trial lawyer. At thirty-four years of age she has traveled the world and is totally independent. Beaker's thirty-five, lives alone in a studio apartment in Germantown, and, oh yes, like Annie, he loves his mother. He's a good guy. His real name is Reginald Lansing. I like Beaker.

"On my way," I say with dread and hang up.

Breathe, for God's sake. I've got to keep it together. *Think of something else.* I pull out, trying to defrost my windshield while dodging the early morning cars parked on my treelined street and tell myself to focus. All I need is to cause an accident this morning because I'm freaking out over this impending verdict. Well, that and the damn email. I scan the neighborhood. It's quiet. *Calm down, you got this. Remember, one thing at a time.* I inhale and slowly exhale. I stop at the light, then turn right onto the main road. I manage to clear my head enough to take in the scenery. I do love living in the heart of the Highlands, a neighborhood so full of flavor, so full of life. Besides a breathtakingly beautiful park, there's something for everyone. I head down Bardstown Road, the main artery that divides residences to the east and the west of the city. Vintage consignment shops, eccentric boutiques, and retail shops are aplenty. Here in this cultural mecca are bookstores, restaurants of diverse ethnicities, night clubs, tattoo parlors, bakeries, and churches of every denomination. Gorgeous older homes surround the park, like the Barnstable Brown residence that annually hosts the Derby Eve gala for celebrities. There are blocks and blocks of Victorian and Georgian style homes in various states of repair. Some are single-family dwellings, while others have been divided into apartment units. Arts and crafts houses—many literally ordered through the old Sears and Roebucks catalogs a hundred years ago and brought in on rail cars, then built on purchased lots—surround the densely populated area, along with bungalows and shotgun houses. City buses navigate up and down the streets, wobbling back and forth on massive steel frames picking up and dropping off passengers. The smell of exhaust is in the air. And the people, oh, the people. This neighborhood was once home to the provocative author Hunter S. Thompson and the astronomer Edwin Hubble. I have a habit of collecting bits of useless trivia that rattle around in my brain. But this place has a history and personality like no other. I belong here because everybody does. On any given day, you can see kids and adults with pink hair, tattoos, and piercings. Some are gay, some bisexual, some transgender, but many are straight. Old hippies walk arm in arm wearing Birkenstocks. Millennial parents are ever-present hauling backpacks and pushing their little ones in state-of-the-art strollers that must require tutorials on how to operate. They take their toddlers to their Montessori day cares or music classes, stopping off on their way home for a flat white or chai tea with soymilk. A potpourri of religions can be found in our community. Catholics and Methodists, Presbyterians and Baptists, as well as the Islamic and Buddhist faiths to name just a few that are practiced here. We are a brilliant kaleidoscope of races and ethnicities—Black, White, Hispanic, Asian, Indian, and a dash of so much more. It's not uncommon to see homeless men and women pushing grocery carts filled to the brim with their earthly possessions. Hipsters rush by, never looking up from their phones. Even refugee men, women, and children find safe harbor here thanks to our neighborhood ministries. The Highlands is home to the wealthiest of the wealthy, the middle class, the poorer residents, the homeless, and the weirdest of weird. In this neighborhood, my age and economic means both fall right of center on the demographic spectrum. I'm a widow in my thirtieth year as a defense attorney. I own a drafty Victorian right behind my favorite bookstore. I've had plans to renovate my house since the day Annie and I moved in. She had just turned four, and we celebrated with cheese pizza on paper plates, sitting on the living room floor among all the boxes. It was a bittersweet time. Celebrating our new lives in this beautiful old house, but unable to share it with him. Joe had only been gone a year before we moved in, a massive heart attack at thirty-nine years old. Annie and I were lost without him. The house was our new beginning, helping us to heal. It seems like forever ago. And as far as those renovations, I did paint the mailbox red. That's a start.

Traffic isn't too awful, but I keep hitting every red light there is from here to the courthouse. Luckily, downtown Louisville is no more than twenty-five minutes from the house. I finally arrive and park in the garage, and the click of my heels echo in the underground. I get through security quickly and show my photo ID. I'm doing great on time and am navigating the gauntlet until I find one of the three elevators is out of order and the others are hovering on the twelfth and fifteenth floors.

"Oh, for Christ's sake," I say out of exasperation. "Sorry." I mumble to the small group waiting behind me for the elevator. I push the button several more times, finally losing all patience. "Aw, screw it!" I head for the steps.

Taking two at a time, I manage to make it to the sixth floor without breaking a heel. My heart is hammering in my chest, more from anxiety than exertion, though I am a bit winded. I stop and catch my breath. *Slow down*, I tell myself. *Keep it together*. I see that reporters and television cameras have gathered. I keep my head down and keep moving as the reporters hurl their questions at me. *How are you feeling about the trial? Do you believe your client will have a guilty verdict? Will you appeal if she's found guilty?* I ignore all of it and enter the courtroom. The prosecution's already there. That arrogant little prick Jack Hamilton, lead prosecutor, flashes his cocky grin at me. It doesn't help that he's dating Annie. *Ugh!* He's incredibly handsome, I'll admit, with that thick ash-blond hair and a gleaming smile. How can anyone's teeth be that white? Looks like he should be in a friggin' toothpaste commercial instead of here playing lawyer. It makes me nuts when I watch some of the women on the jury, regardless of their age, blush when he flashes that smile in their direction. I mean, seriously, I'd like to slap that Ivy League grin right off his face. He's a Stanford grad who sailed through with a full ride, even though his extremely rich parents could have easily afforded tuition anywhere. Years ago, I graduated from The University of Louisville, for both undergraduate and law school, bartending at night in the early years to survive. As a single mother, I worked hard to provide for my daughter. I didn't do too badly, eventually opening my own practice and sending my daughter to Vanderbilt so she could take her place as a member of the firm. I look over at that smug face and give him the finger, and he responds with a full-blown smile.

"Is that any way for you to treat your future son-in-law?" he says, giving me a wink.

"You are delusional, counselor," I say loud enough for all to hear.

"And a good morning to you, too," he volleys back, still wearing that irritating grin.

I disregard him. I set my purse and satchel down and take my seat at the defense table, peeling off my coat and throwing it on the back of my chair. Beaker arrives and gives me a double thumbs up as he takes the seat directly behind me. The side door opens, and in walks Emma Davies, escorted by the jailer. She is rail thin and looks as if she hasn't eaten in weeks. There are shadows under her eyes, shadows that have increased exponentially since the trial began. Her thick, short wavy hair remains dark, only slightly graying, which is not unusual for those of us in our early sixties. She must have been an aging beauty, but since all of this began, the lines on her face have deepened. Her soft brown eyes are weary. Even still, she's lovely. Her positive attitude has been remarkable throughout the trial. It all seems quite ridiculous. This tiny wisp of a woman stands accused of killing her boss, J.D. Bauer, and his wife Margaret in their own home. Mr. Bauer was one of Louisville's wealthiest businessmen. He was the CFO of Elite Wealth Management, one of the largest financial conglomerates in the U.S. According to Emma, Mr. Bauer asked her to stop by his house and pick up some signed papers needed for a meeting later in the day that he would not be able to attend. He and his wife were catching a flight that afternoon for Paris to celebrate their thirtieth wedding anniversary. Emma arrived late in the morning, picked up the papers, and delivered them back to the office. Somewhere between the time she left the Bauers' residence and the thirty minutes it took her to get back to the office, the Bauers were killed. Both had been shot. Forensics would later prove that both the husband and wife were shot with Mr. Bauer's own gun. The problem? The gun was located about a foot from his body. His clothing did have traces of gun residue, but there was nothing at all on Emma's clothes that morning. There was no DNA evidence to convict her and no motive. The prosecution painted her as a woman scorned. According to office gossip, Emma provided her boss with more than her expert office skills behind closed doors and would constantly stay late with him to "catch up" on things. There had been other rumors that she and Mr. Bauer had had a long-term relationship. But there was no direct evidence of that either. She should never have been charged in the first place. At least I hope the jury sees it that way. Emma takes her seat next to me.

"Good morning," she says with a nervous smile. "It's good to see you."

I stare at her. She greets me as if she's meeting me for coffee, instead of to learn her fate. "It's good to see you too, Emma," I whisper. I cover her hand with mine and look deep into her eyes. "Stay strong. I'm here for you."

"Oh, Bertie," she says placing her hand over mine, "I know that."

I look at her, and I'm moved by her strength. I'm wondering if I'll have that kind of resilience to face whatever's coming my way. I desperately try and put on a brave face for her.

"Just hold on tight to my hand, okay?"

She nods. "You've done all you can. It's out of our hands and into the good Lord's." She looks back and searches for her son in the courtroom. She finds him and blows him a kiss.

I secretly pray the good Lord is sitting in one of those juror's seats, 'cause we could use divine intervention right about now. As if on cue, the jury enters the courtroom, and I quickly study their faces, looking for any signs of what's to come. Some glance our way, others look down, which could mean something or nothing. I don't know. I can't read them. I look at Emma and give her my best smile. She smiles back and continues to grip my hand. It's almost as if our situation is reversed. She's consoling me. I marvel at this woman.

"All rise. The Honorable Joseph Edwards presiding," says the courtroom deputy. Judge Edwards has been on the bench for as long as I can remember. There are far worse judges a lawyer could argue a case in front of. He's been fair and consistent throughout the trial. He's a no-nonsense judge and doesn't put up with any shenanigans—his words. I help Emma rise, wrapping my arm around her for balance and support, as much for me as for her.

"You may be seated," says the judge. "It is my understanding that the jury has reached a verdict." He's directing his statement to the middle-aged man who has been selected by the jury as the foreperson.

"We have, your honor."

"Would you please hand the verdict to the court deputy?"

Judge Edwards silently reads the verdict, his face a total blank slate. He hands the verdict back to the foreperson.

"Would the defendant please rise?"

We rise together.

"Would the foreperson please read the verdict?"

"We, the jury, find the defendant, Emma Margaret Davies NOT GUILTY."

Someone seated in the chambers lets out a gasp. At first, there's no other sound. Time seems to stand still. I'm frozen. I can't speak. The sounds of both shock and jubilation can be heard in the courtroom. It jars me from my stupor. I look at Emma. She looks to be in a trance. Our hands are bound together in a grip so tight that there's practically no blood flow. We've both been holding our breath. I'm finally able to get some words out.

"Emma, congratulations! We did it, we did it. You're free." I grab her in a bear hug, wrapping my arms around her tiny frame.

I finally release her. She's smiling sadly. A tear rolls down her face. I reach out and wipe it away with the back of my hand. "It's okay, you're free to go. It's over. It's all over, Emma."

"It's over, it's really over," she whispers.

"Yes, Emma, it is, it's over. You can go home. And I think I see your ride," I say as her son and daughter-in-law approach.

"Thank you, Bertie. Thank you," she says tearfully. We take a moment to give hugs all around. I watch as her son leads his mother out of the courtroom and into freedom. *Happy endings*, I think, *so few and far between.*

"Congratulations, Counselor," says Jack with an outstretched hand.

"Thank you." I accept his congratulatory handshake. I grab my coat and briefcase and turn to exit.

"Congratulations, Bertie," Beaker says giving me a fist bump.

"Thanks," I say. "Hey, listen, I'll see you back in the office in a bit."

"Yeah. Hey, you okay? Cheer up! We won, remember?" Beaker says as he raises his clenched fists in the air, shaking them as a sign of victory.

I smile. Beaker's not exactly emotionally in tune with what others may be feeling. That makes me appreciate his efforts. It's a stretch for him. Before leaving the courthouse, I take a few minutes to give a brief statement to the press. "Yes, we are very pleased with the verdict," and "I never had a doubt that the jury would find my client not guilty."

I don't know if my outward appearance reveals my inner turmoil. I make it to the bathroom, locking myself in a stall. Thank God I'm alone. I collapse onto the toilet seat. I don't have the luxury of celebrating the win for Emma. It begins as a quiet sob, then crescendos into crashing waves of pent-up fear and anxiety. I stretch out my arms, reaching my palms to the walls of the stall for balance. It's all just been too much. And it's only just begun for me. I will myself to get my act together, but the words in the email keep flashing in my brain. *Can we meet?* It's probably just one of the "Fireflies" reaching out, right? Or maybe there's someone else seeking justice or revenge? Today I'm the defense attorney, but how long before I'm the defendant? I rack my brain, going through a list of possibilities and realize it's a lesson in futility. I can suspect all I want, but I won't know until whoever it is reveals themselves. Maybe someone's been patient all these years, just waiting for the right time to strike. Is this some psychological game they're playing, to push me to react out of fear and...and...WHAT? My thoughts are running completely wild.

"Stop it, stop it," I hiss through clenched teeth while pressing my fingertips to my temples. I close my eyes and rub my temples until the pounding in my head eases and my breathing begins to return to normal. I use the john, blow my nose, and regain enough composure to stand up and exit the stall. I look in the mirror. I resemble something feral, like a racoon. I clean up the best I can, wiping the mascara from under my eyes with a moistened paper towel. My face has no color. I apply a bit of lipstick and even rub some into my cheeks. Better, but still not great. I run a comb through my out-of-control mane and knot my hair at the base of my neck as best I can with a clip I find at the bottom of my purse. I give a last look in the mirror and square my shoulders. *It's time to go.*

On the drive back to the office, I'm exhausted, like I've swallowed an anchor and weigh about a thousand pounds. I look at my watch, and it's not even noon. I take a moment to think about Emma and silently thank my higher power for granting her liberty. She's lucky. She's free to go anywhere, travel anywhere, and I'm elated for her, I truly am. I'm mean, hell, I wish I was her right now. I'm not quite ready to go back to the office, not just yet. On impulse I pull into Starbucks. I sit in the car listening to the radio, wondering what my next move will be. I finally turn off the engine and enter the coffee shop, ordering a tall coffee of the day, no room for cream. I sit at a table up front, sipping the scalding hot caffeine, watching traffic pass by. I take out my phone, anxiously checking my emails, but there's still nothing. I take another sip and watch as an extremely well put together woman walks in with her daughter. How do I know it's her daughter? The young girl is the spitting image of her mother. I wonder why this girl's not in school. Maybe they're coming back from the dentist or a doctor's appointment. Like her mother, she's got a remarkable face, flawless skin. Her long blond ponytail trails down her back. She's wearing a navy sweater, a white button-down blouse tucked into a navy and dark-green plaid pleated skirt. It's obviously a school uniform, and if I were to guess, I'd say she's around twelve or thirteen. They wait in line to give their orders. The girl's chatting incessantly to her mother, while her mother nods periodically. I wonder what it would have been like to have a mother like that. Though I can't quite make out the conversation, I can hear the girl's lyrical intonations, and I see the animation on her face as she relays to her mother the colorful details of what is most likely her latest adolescent drama. I continue watching over the brim of my coffee cup as the girl waves her hands in the air and vacillates between intermittent bursts of laughter and the rapid fire of enthusiastic dialogue. Like girls do. Like we did when we were young.

1969

TWO

Estill County, Kentucky

None of us really wants to be here. There just isn't much else to do. When you're twelve in Estill County, your options on a Friday night are slim. Anyway, most of us attend the same school, but not the same church. You can swing a cat in Estill County and hit a church. Like me, some of us live in Ravenna, others in Irvine. These towns are just two sides of the same coin that make up Estill County. It doesn't really matter which side of the coin you live on, 'cause we all attend the same junior high. Well, the only junior high. Next year, we'll attend Estill County High. But in school, we pretty much stick with kids who live on our side of the coin. Tonight's lock-in is compliments of the Catholics. I'm feeling nervous standing here with my pillow and rolled-up pink comforter under my arm. My eyes scan the large meeting hall, looking for friendly faces. My friend Audrey is supposed to be here, but I don't see her.

"What's your name?" asks the plump lady in the loud flowery blouse. I can't help but stare. Her bangs look as if someone sneezed while cutting her hair. I try not to laugh. She has a clipboard in her sausage fingers. I'm guessing she's a church member who's chaperoning for the night.

"Uh, Beatrice Campbell, but everyone calls me Bertie," I say.

"Oh! Bertie *Campbell*," she says, with a little too much emphasis on the *Campbell*. She may not know me by sight, but she sure knows the name. I'm used to it. Mama's got quite a reputation around here. Finding my name on the list, she checks me off. "Go find a spot against the wall over there and drop your things." She points to the left. "Then come back over here to the bleachers and take a seat." I can feel her eyes follow me as I walk away.

I stop and look around as high-pitched squeals emit from a couple of the girls I recognize but don't like, followed by raucous laughter from some obnoxious boys they're trying to impress. This only adds to my exasperation. I don't want to be here. I'm not seeing anyone I normally hang out with, so I'm thinking the best thing to do is just walk myself right outta here.

I turn to leave when I hear Audrey's voice. "Hey, Bertie, where you goin'? You're not leaving, are you? Sorry I'm late. Daddy made me feed the boys before I could leave."

I turn around to see Audrey Smallwood with her flaming head of hair making a beeline toward me. I couldn't be more relieved to see anyone in my whole life. Audrey's responsible for her two younger brothers, since her mother died of breast cancer last year. Her daddy, like so many men in Ravenna, works for the railroad and he isn't home too much, leaving Audrey to do almost all the chores around the house. *Thank goodness! I'm not alone.* "Oh, hey, no, just trying to figure out where I need to go," I lie.

"I think we're supposed to dump our stuff over there. C'mon!" she says.

I follow. I'm not exactly shy, but in school we stay pretty much in our own cliques. It's odd to see kids from school at a church lock-in. I'm not a member of this church. Well, I'm not really a member of any church. Mama's not exactly the church-going kind, so I feel even weirder attending anything connected with the spiritual side of town. Mama made me come tonight. Believe me when I say she wasn't looking out for my social well-being, but for her own. Like always, she's got plans, usually engaging in at least three of the seven deadly sins, and those plans don't include me.

There's now a crowd of boys and girls gathering on the bleachers. A piano has been shoved back against the wall. I figure the church probably uses this room for choir practice among other things, like potluck suppers, bereavements, and meetings. Audrey and I take a seat. The youth director, Mr. Baldwin, asks us all to get quiet and settle ourselves down as a handful of boys rambunctiously bounce around the top of the bleachers playing a dangerous game of King of the Hill. Mr. Baldwin looks a bit nervous as he removes his handkerchief from his back pocket and wipes his brow and neck before introducing himself, then introducing the lady with the crazy bangs, Mrs. Crenshaw, Bobby Crenshaw's mother. Bobby's sitting at the top of the bleachers with his friends. He ducks his head when his mom is introduced. His friends elbow him in the ribs. They whoop and holler, trying hard to embarrass him more than he already is. Bobby's face is tomato red.

"That's enough. You boys settle yourselves down. We appreciate Mrs. Crenshaw giving of her time. Now, y'all just quiet down, you hear me?" Baldwin repeats. When he feels it's sufficiently quiet, he leads us in a prayer, followed by the "do's and don'ts" of the evening's lock-in. No physical contact between boys and girls, no leaving the hall without permission—only to use the bathroom. No smoking, cursing, or fighting. No playing or banging on the piano...the list goes on. Jeez, so many rules for simply having pizza, listening to music, and playing board games.

"Well, are we even allowed to talk to each other? Why are we even here if we can't have a little fun?" says Marie

Parker, the prettiest and most popular girl that goes to our school. She lives in Irvine. I in no way move in her circles.

We all laugh. She's just said what we're all thinking.

"Well, of course you'll be able to talk and have fun, Marie, but we have to have rules," said Baldwin, adjusting his horn-rimmed glasses. It's obvious he knows Marie and her family well. The Parker clan, a Catholic family with seven kids, are members of this parish. I'm not surprised Marie would be the one to speak up. She's always trying to get attention. She's a bit boy crazy. I glance over and see Eddy Dennison is seated directly behind her. He's practically the male version of Marie, meaning the loudest and most popular boy in school. I don't like him. Yeah, he's cute, but he's a bully, so I do my best to avoid him. He's always picking on kids. I saw him knock Billy Stiver's lunch tray right out of his hands one day in the school cafeteria. Billy ended up wearing his chili on his shirt. Eddy sat and laughed while Billy was made to clean up the mess by order of the P.E. teacher, Mr. Johnson. It was unfair. Eddy's a head taller than

Billy and outweighs him by at least twenty-five pounds. The fact that Eddy's on the basketball team gets him special treatment. Billy's just a scrawny little kid who goes straight home after school to help tend his family's farm. Eddy sickens me. He really does. As I said before, I avoid him.

We sit on the bleachers for another fifteen minutes, not really listening to Mr. Baldwin. Finally, the meeting is adjourned, and we're released to officially begin "the fun." Audrey and I find a couple of other girls to hang with and spend the next few hours sitting cross-legged on the floor gossiping about boys and teachers, playing Uno, eating pizza, and drinking soda. Surprisingly, I'm having fun. It's close to midnight when we hear the laughter. There's something happening.

"C'mon, let's go see what' going on," Audrey says. We get up to follow. There's a crowd forming in the back of the meeting hall, and it's hard to see over the heads of some of the kids. We move around to the other side to get a better look.

Kids are laughing and pointing at a girl. She's a petite little thing with shoulder-length brown hair. She's standing practically in the corner and even though her head is down, I recognize her immediately. It's Eve Henderson who's in both my art and English classes. That girl can flat-out draw and write too, poems and stories and stuff. Teachers are always talking about how talented she is, but she's a rather odd girl. Maybe it's because she's more gifted than the rest of us and she doesn't quite fit in. I'm surprised to see her here because she pretty much keeps to herself. In fact, I don't remember seeing her hang around much with anyone at school; she even eats lunch by herself. I'm not sure what's happening, as I scan the collective mob trying to figure out what's so funny. Some are doubled over laughing, while others are shrieking and pointing in Eve's direction. It doesn't take me long to realize what they're laughing about. Eve's wearing a pair of white shorts, and they're stained crimson around her upper thighs and private area. She's obviously started her period tonight and the shame and humiliation of it is written all over her face.

"Look, she's bleeding like a slaughtered pig," Eddy says laughing and falling over himself. The crowd roars with maniacal laughter. He starts squealing like a pig, trying to get more of a rise out of the group and rain more verbal abuse, if possible, down on Eve. "We should start calling her Tampon," Eddy says, entertaining the crowd.

"Oh my God, that's so gross!" one of the girls screeches.

I look over to see Mr. Baldwin and Mrs. Crenshaw standing behind the crowd, smiling and shaking their heads, as if this is just silly stuff kids do. I can't believe it. They're just standing there, letting this poor girl be publicly crucified.

Audrey and I look at each other. "C'mon, let's help her," I say. Audrey nods to affirm she's with me. Together we push our way through the group to reach Eve. However, to our surprise, we aren't the first to come to her defense.

Marie steps in and turns on the crowd with a vengeance. "Y'all ought to be ashamed of yourselves. You boys are actin' like fools. All of you need to shut the hell up. Y'all are so danged immature. Maybe your mommas haven't explained them facts of life to you yet. And you girls, how dare you laugh! You think she's the only one who gets a period each month? You're probably just jealous 'cause she's showin' signs of bein' a woman. Y'all probably haven't gotten your monthly curse yet. I'll bet you can't even fill out a training bra without stuffin' 'em with Kleenex." The boys are now whistling and laughing at her stings. The girls are smiling, but it's obvious they're embarrassed to be called out by the most popular girl in school.

I grab my blanket off the floor and wrap it around Eve. Audrey and I stand on either side of her. Marie stands directly in front of her, daring anyone to say another word. In that moment, I knew there was more to this girl than I realized.

"Okay, everybody, show's over. It's time for y'all to go back to your places," says Mr. Baldwin.

"C'mon, Eve, let's get you to the bathroom," I say.

"I've got a tampon in my purse," says Audrey. "Ugh, sorry," she says, realizing that's the name Eddy just used on Eve. "I mean, I'll go get it."

I wince at the mention of the word *tampon*. Surely it will now be Eddy's new pet name for Eve and there's likely no escaping it.

"Don't worry none, Eve. They won't mess with you no more," says Marie. "I'll make sure of it. We're going to get you the hell outta here."

Eve still hasn't said a word. Like a sheep, she simply follows us across the meeting hall, the blanket dragging behind her.

Present Day

THREE

My phone rings, interrupting my thoughts. It's Annie.

"Hi, sweetie," I say as cheerfully as I can.

"Hi there, I hear congratulations are in order. I'm so sorry I wasn't there this morning when the verdict came in. I guess Beaker told you I had a deposition scheduled in the Martin case."

"Oh yeah, no worries. Yes, it was really something. I'm so happy for Emma."

"What's she going to do now?" Annie asked.

"Anything she damn well pleases," I say with a forced laugh.

"Well, Jack said you did a wonderful job with the case, even though he's pretty bummed he lost."

"Well, I'm sure it won't be long before he's given a fresh victim to try. He'll be back in front of the cameras in no time."

"Now, Mom, that's not fair. Why don't you like him?"

"Oh, I don't know, Annie. Maybe it's because I get the feeling everything comes so easy for him, maybe it's because he continually wears that pious look on his face, or maybe I find his particular brand of arrogance off-putting. Take your pick."

"On what basis do you draw all those conclusions about him?"

"On my gut basis. It rarely fails me."

"You'd really like him if you'd get to know him. We ought to all go out to dinner sometime. Which reminds me, I'm having lunch with him in about an hour, so I'll see you in the office later."

"Swell, have a nice lunch," I reply on a flat note. She knows down deep inside that I respect and support any decisions she makes for herself. Jack Hamilton, however, gets in my crawl. I've raised Annie to be an independent thinker. She's got brains and is a good judge of character, for the most part.

"I'll tell Jack you asked about him," she says, chiding me.

"He'll know you're lying. Is that any way to build an honest relationship? On falsehoods?" I immediately feel a stab of guilt and regret making the comment. "No, really, enjoy your lunch," I say, wearily.

"Mom, you okay? You sound strange."

I've never been able to keep much from my daughter. We can read each other well, and we both know when something's not right. I do my best to keep her from worrying. "Yes, sweetie, I'm fine. Just a bit tired. This trial's taken the starch out of me. Nothing a little rest won't fix. I just need some time to maybe catch my breath."

"You know, Mom, you should do exactly that."

"Exactly what?"

"Get some rest, take some time for yourself. Let Beaker and me handle things for a while. I'll bet Dolores could do some of the small stuff."

I challenge her remark. "What are you talking about? Dolores can still do the big stuff." But if I'm honest, I've been concerned with little things I'm noticing. I hired Dolores Bell fifteen years ago. She was one of the first female attorneys in the state of Kentucky and had practiced for years at one of the leading firms in Louisville. An unfortunate stroke left her with some mobility issues and speech difficulties, to the extent that she could no longer try cases. After all those years of service, she walked away, having negotiated a generous severance package for herself. But Dolores wasn't ready to give up law altogether. She clomped into my office riding her cane one day and scared the hell out of me, her approach so direct it stunned me. Not only was her physical size intimidating, but her autocratic disposition left no doubt as to who was in charge. She didn't even wait to ask if I was busy. She barged in like a cyclone and proceeded to tell me that she was the best damn lawyer I'd ever have the privilege of working with. Oh, and that she'd work cheap. She went on to say that she was impressed with my work, and that impressing her wasn't easy to do. I laughed. Who the hell is this woman coming in here and telling me that I'm "good enough" to work with her? Well, she's a legend is who she is. Not only was she one of the first women criminal defense attorneys in the state of Kentucky, but she's won every single case she ever tried. That's who she was. I wasn't stupid. I was a struggling attorney who could barely pay my law clerk. I seriously couldn't believe my good fortune—well, even though her caustic nature was a price I had to pay. Dolores's speech may have taken a hit in the early days after the stroke, but even today she has one of the sharpest legal minds I've encountered. She just turned eighty-two years young. She told us the only way we'll get her out of here is on angel wings. She drinks whiskey straight, bets the horses—well, bets on anything—is addicted to pie, and always says what's on her mind. Whether you want to hear it or not. She rarely falters now when speaking. We love our ornery, bullish barrister, horns and all. She takes an Uber to and from her condo, coming in around nine a.m. and leaving around two p.m. to avoid traffic. Like me, she's a resident of the Highlands and lives in one of the nicest buildings in the neighborhood, The 1400 Willows. It's wonderful having her so close. On many evenings, I'll bring her dinner or pick her up and take her out. She celebrates holidays and birthdays with us. She's practically a grandmother to Annie—a cranky one, and a great friend and mentor to me, even if she's a pain in the ass most of the time.

"Well, will you at least think about it?" Annie persists.

"I'll think about it. See you later, sweetie. Love you!"

"Bye, Mom. Love you too!"

I look at my phone and realize I've been sitting in Starbucks for far too long. I throw my empty cup away and glance back at the mother/daughter duo now seated nearby. The young girl's licking whipped cream off the straw of her Frappuccino. They look content, happy. I smile and hope they remain as close as they seem to be at this very moment.

It's just before noon when I reach the office. B. Dunnigan Law Offices are located literally in the back of Blue's Diner on Main Street. I think it was fate that brought me to Blue's twenty-five years ago. I had spent the better part of a soggy, wet day searching downtown Louisville for a place to lease. After Joe died, I wanted to get away from the firm where we'd met and worked together before we got married. Joe left the firm shortly before we tied the knot and accepted a job in the county attorney's office, but even though he'd moved on from the office where we'd both worked, I continuously felt Joe Dunnigan's presence in every corner of that place. After he died, those feelings intensified, and I just couldn't stay any longer. There were just too many memories, and I wanted to try and leave some of the sorrow behind and venture out to fulfill my dream of opening my own practice. So, on that dreary, rain-drenched afternoon, I was on a mission, regardless of the weather. I was tired and starving when I spotted Blue's Diner from the other side of the street. I didn't think I could walk much further because my feet were absolutely killing me, and I was soaked and needed food. The owner, Maisie Chandler, was behind the counter. She greeted me with the biggest smile I'd ever seen.

"You look like you could use a little something, maybe even a towel," she said with a laugh, handing me a large napkin to wipe the rain dripping from my nose.

"I sure can. Thanks so much. I'm starving."

"Well, you swim on over there, and we'll get you fixed right up."

And she did, handing me an extra napkin and a menu. It took me all of thirty seconds to zero in on what I wanted. It was one of the best open-faced roast beef sandwiches I'd ever put in my mouth. And the lemon meringue pie was to die for, just tart enough and a whole lotta sweet. Since it was later in the afternoon, there were few customers in the place. Maisie came over with the coffee pot, refilled my cup, and, before long, I invited her to sit and chat. She was a sweetheart. I told her I was looking for space to rent for my law office.

She just laughed and said, "You mean you didn't see the sign in the window?" I asked her what sign. That's when she walked over to the front window, pulled the curtain back, and turned the sign around. *SPACE FOR RENT*. It was one of those surreal moments. I asked her if I might be in an episode of *The Twilight Zone*. She just laughed and said, "Oh Lord, I used to have such a crush on Rod Serling."

Maisie died several years ago. Her daughter Missy and her husband own the diner now. It's a win-win for all of us. I just signed the lease for another five years. I could move to one of the more modern buildings downtown, but why? It wouldn't be cost effective, but more importantly, we're all happy right where we are. It also reminds me of another time, another diner, giving me the chance to think back fondly and smile.

I wave to Missy as I pass through the front dining room. She's got her hands full clearing a table for a group of customers waiting to be seated. Up front is set up like most diners, with booths lining one wall and tables for four peppering the rest of the space. The front counter has a glass display case that's filled with candy, gum, and other enticing items—those impulse buys you'd most likely grab on your way out. I don't always wait until I'm leaving to get my fix of M&M's, it wouldn't be out of the question for me to visit the counter at ten a.m. for chocolate. I'm not the slightest bit ashamed of indulging my weakness in the morning. This place is like a journey through time. There's even an antique cash register, complete with brass buttons and a bell that rings after every purchase. Enter the next room, and you've stepped into Grandma's house, where green ivy creeps along cream-colored nicotine-stained wallpaper, the paper sticky in places and peeling at the seams. A massive oak antique hutch practically takes up the entire wall. The long dining table is made of the same rich oak as the hutch and consumes two-thirds of the room. It seats ten or more, accommodating larger parties. Two smaller wooden tables with matching chairs are off to the side, and a heavy iron chandelier hangs from the center of the room. Its spikey leaves hold up eight luminaries, and its base resembles a massive acorn. I can't say this place is pretty, but it's homey. The building's well over a hundred years old, and its bones rest in one of downtown Louisville's best locations. It's minutes from hotels, museums, restaurants, and the performing arts. I love—well, we—love it here. Our offices are located down the hall, just beyond the "acorn room" as I like to call it. We have a sum total of three rooms: my office, Annie's office, and a large conference room/office that Beaker and Dolores share. Our bathrooms are communal, including with diner customers. We usually enter through the front of the diner because it's easier to access from the parking garage. However, there's a back entrance that comes in handy from time to time.

I pass the kitchen as I make my way to my office, the smell of fried bacon filling the air. Before I even reach the office, I hear their voices. It's Beaker and Dolores in a spirited conversation; her deep raspy voice carries like a baritone. I enter and take in the scene. Beaker's hoisted himself onto the conference table, swinging his feet, as Dolores schools him on the horses that are running in next month's Derby. Dolores is seated at her computer, her wide girth taking up the entire space of the chair we had specially made for her, for comfort and ease of getting up. She's looking at racing stats online. Dolores has attended every Kentucky Derby since 1962, except for 2004, when she had her stroke. She has her own private box at Churchill Downs, which is an incredible social feat in and of itself, not to mention a hat for every Run for the Roses she's attended. That's forty-one hats. She's witnessed three Triple Crown winners—Secretariat in 1973, Affirmed in 1978, and American Pharaoh in 2015. We all know the dates because she's never let us forget them. I've only seen one of those winners, and she never fails to remind me. She can tell you more about the Kentucky horsing industry and its history than anyone I know. We've had the great fortune of being her Derby guests these past several years. This year's no exception. She's once again extended the invitation to all, but for now, well, who knows what my circumstances will be, come Derby Day?

"Okay, what am I paying you guys for?" I say laughing, trying to appear as much like myself as possible. "Never mind," I say holding my hands up. "I gotta get these heels off. I'll be right back." I hobble to my office, taking my shoes off along the way. I grab my Nikes out of my desk drawer and throw the torturous heels in. I'm done with those for the day. I carry my running shoes back to the conference table and sit.

"Can you believe it? As many times as I've gone over this, this boy still doesn't know what a trifecta is," Dolores exclaims.

"Says the woman who thought she could get sick catching a computer virus," Beaker replies.

Dolores lets out a hoot of laughter, and then proceeds to cough uncontrollably. I worry about that hack she's acquired.

"Oh, you two!" I say shaking my head.

She finally catches her breath. "Well, lady, congratulations on the Davies trial. See, I told you to use that closing argument, didn't I?"

"Yes, you did. Thank you, Dolores. What size and font would you like me to order your *I told you so* banner in?" I ask, looking up as I tie my shoes.

"Oh, darlin', you don't have to do that. Just get me a bottle of Pappy Van Winkle," she says with a grin.

"Uh, no! That's more than a month of your salary. Try again."

"Oh, hell, forget it. I'll let you have that piece of winning advice for free this time." She dismisses me with a wave of her hand.

"Thanks ever-so-much, Dolores."

I turn my attention to Beaker. "Any messages?"

"Just a few. I left them on your desk. Brian Kramer called and said he'd schedule the hearing in the Alfred case for some time in May. Um...Mrs. Donnelly cancelled tomorrow's appointment. She'll try and schedule something with you next week. I told her we'd get back with her. And that's it. Uh, no, wait, there was one more. Kind of an odd call. Some woman called asking for you, but she wouldn't leave her name. Said to tell you that she knows where your green box can be found, or something to the effect. She said she'd be back in touch, then she hung up."

I can't hide the shock on my face.

"Bertie, you okay?" Beaker says, hopping down from the table. "What's wrong? You look scared stiff."

Dolores looks up from the computer. "Bertie, what's the matter? Who was that?" she asks, looking over the rim of her glasses.

I sit there, unable to respond. My brain's on hold. I open my mouth to speak. "N-n-n...nobody, I dunno who she is. I mean, I haven't the foggiest idea. Listen," I say trying to recover, "I just remembered something I forgot to do. I gotta go."

"Bertie, what is it?" Beaker asks again.

"Beaker, help Dolores into her Uber this afternoon. Uh....it's nothing, it's really no big deal. I just promised somebody I'd do something for them, and it completely slipped my mind. I'll call you later." I don't wait for them to ask any more questions. I run back to my office and grab the messages left on my desk. I find the one I'm looking for. I have yet to take off my coat, so I shove the note in my pocket.

Everything's a blur as I quickly exit the diner. Missy's quite possibly saying something to me, but the blood is rushing in my ears and I don't stop. Cool air strikes my face. I shove my hand into my pocket, feeling the note practically burning my fingers. I walk/run. I need to think. I reach the next block and head north toward the river, taking the walkway to the viewing area that overlooks the Ohio. I end my escape at the railing, gripping it to steady myself. I look out over the choppy water. It's muddy and the river's up. Tree branches large and small are bobbing their limbs in and out, riding the currents at a rapid speed. I watch the cars and trucks pass over the Kennedy Bridge, connecting Kentucky and Indiana. Strands of hair escape and whip at my face. It's a shock to think someone knows about the box. How is that even possible? Somebody from back home, they most certainly know. I hold the message over the railing and let it go, watching it as the wind carries it away.

1975

FOUR

Estill County, Kentucky

I carefully count out the bills, making sure they're all there. I count them twice for good measure before placing them back in the faded green tin I keep hidden in the loose floorboards of my closet. The decades-old tin is beginning to rust in the corners. The tiny box is covered in cherry blossoms and the lid is crowned with a finial-like knob of brushed gold. The tin itself isn't important—it's what's inside. It is both my freedom and my revenge. Six hundred and seventy-three dollars and forty-seven cents. I've been saving that money for what seems like an eternity. She won't find it this time. Mama might stumble around in her drunken stupor looking for it, but she's too lazy to sift through the piles of dirty underwear, bras, and shoes that litter my creaky closet floor. I was fooled once by her, but never again. Until last year, I kept my money in a savings account I proudly opened at the bank in Irvine, but Mama had sweet-talked that sleazy branch manager into allowing her access to my account. He was just one of the many married men Glennis Campbell was sleeping with. Mama had gone to the bank and cleaned out my account, taking every last dime I had saved from my waitressing job at the Good Eats diner. I was already handing over some of my weekly wages ever since I started there. But the money I shared from hours on my feet waiting tables wasn't enough for her; she wanted it all. I bitterly think back to the day I discovered my mother's betrayal. Searing pan-fried anger burns through me even now just thinking about it. I remember it as clear as yesterday. I had stopped at the bank on a Friday afternoon to deposit my check.

"You do realize that your account contains zero funds?" said Mrs. Avery, the piggish-faced, gray-haired sourpuss teller behind the counter.

"No, ma'am, that can't be correct. Please check it again," I said firmly, trying to remain calm and respectful.

"I can assure you that your account shows a balance of zero," she said haughtily. "I will be glad to keep the account open if you're planning on depositing that check." She pointed to the check I had with me.

Losing my respectful façade, I bellowed, "This bank has stolen my money, and I demand that it be returned!"

"Young lady, you need to keep your voice down," pig woman whispered in embarrassment as she scanned the bank for customers within earshot.

"I will not keep my voice down!" I yelled at the top of my lungs. "I want my money, and I want it now!"

I was in a panic and causing quite a scene when out of his office came Lloyd Winkle, the sleazebag bank manager with his greasy, slicked-back hair. His bulging belly was protruding from the jacket of his ugly tan polyester suit. I'll never forget the look on his pasty face when he saw me. He turned white and appeared quite flustered. He finally found his composure and said, "Miss Bertie, perhaps you should go home and discuss this with your mother."

Instantly, I knew without a doubt what had happened. I'd caught him a while back slithering down the stairs, having come from Mama's bedroom, carrying his hat and shoes in his hands. He saw me too. The snake! I couldn't believe the audacity—telling me to go home and ask my mama about my own account.

"Mr. Winkle," I stated upon leaving, "you might want to get yourself a shot of penicillin. She's been scratching a whole lot down there lately, if you know what I mean." I pointed in the direction of my crotch. I heard Mrs. Avery's sudden intake of breath. It was apparent by the look on the faces of the few customers still in the bank that I had shocked them too, except for one elderly man who just shook his head and chuckled. It wouldn't be long before the whole town would hear the story. I vowed Mama would pay.

"That bitch," I say, still seething from the memory. I snap the rubber band around the bills and place them in the tin. I look at the other items inside. I smile, thinking about how mad Mama was when she discovered I had taken the tin from her dresser. Served her right, stealing from me. I found it one day when I was looking through her dresser for some of the money she'd stolen. I let a few days go by before I began my search. I wanted her to think I'd let the whole incident slide. She was mistaken. I found the tin tucked away in her bottom drawer, under her silk stockings and slips. Those silk stockings were a reminder of the status she had once held and now lost. Folks in our town of Ravenna used to call our street Silk Stocking Lane, even though it was Fifth Street, 'cause the wives of the big wigs who worked for the Louisville and Nashville railroad could afford silk stockings. My daddy was a big wig engineer years ago. That was before he up and disappeared. Mama is still buying silk stockings, but now she can only purchase those stockings by the work she does mostly on her back. She can't afford them as a cashier at the Bag It in Ravenna. I took the mystery box to my room. I remember sitting cross-legged on the bed, staring at the box in front of me, debating whether to open it. I'd never taken anything that wasn't mine before. In the end, my bitterness overtook my conscience, and I opened it. There was no money inside, but I knew

I'd discovered something far more valuable to Mama. Something so important that she felt the need to hide it.

That was eight months ago. I look down at the contents of the box that's in my possession. What is it they say? "Possession's nine-tenths of the law." Something like that. I didn't find any money in the box that day, but I did find things that Mama treasured and kept hidden. They are now mine. There are two photographs, a red bandana, a small bottle of perfume containing the remnants of an amber liquid, and a small glass jar with a metal screw cap. The jar contains what looks like a lightning bug, one of those little insects that lights up the night. It looks sad and brittle. Who would intentionally incarcerate a defenseless lightning bug? It's cruel. I set the jar aside and pick up one of the photographs. I stare at it again, as I've done ever since I found the secret box. It's a photo of my father. He looks like a man-child, quite handsome, possibly the same age as I am now. He's leaning against a light-colored car, an older model, perhaps a Chevy, or maybe a Ford. He's got a strong, chiseled jaw; a lit cigarette dangles from his mouth.

He's wearing a t-shirt tucked into a pair of form-fitting blue jeans. The other photo's also of him, but there's no mistaking the teenage knockout clinging to him. That's Mama. They're entangled, leaning against the hood of the car. Mama's arms are wrapped around his waist, and her hair is mostly covered with a bandana tied at the top of her head, kinda like that old poster of the lady that hangs in Mr. Gregory's garage. What was her name? Oh yeah, Rosie the Riveter. There's just a peak of Mama's dark curls escaping from the scarf. She's wearing blue jeans, rolled up just above the knees, her tiny waist accentuated by the white blouse knotted around her midriff. These two, my mother and my father, appear to be so happy, so in love. This is the only image I have of them together. I turn the photo over and read the words that I've read so many times before:

Glennis, my light, my firefly. All my love, Jesse

That's it. I'd been told by folks around town that my father, Jesse Ray Campbell, was a handsome, kind, and generous man, but Mama refuses to speak to me about him. He remains a mystery. I pick up the jar and look at the dead lightning bug. Yeah, she was really pissed when she finally discovered her box was missing.

"Beatrice Ray Campbell, you get your ass up here right this minute," Mama screamed from her bedroom upstairs.

I knew it was coming. She called me by my full name. Normally it's just Bertie. I had just come in from work. I slowly entered her room. Mama was standing in front of her dresser, items tossed about in what appeared to be a frantic attempt to search for something. I knew immediately she was drunk.

"What are you doing home from work so early? Your shift isn't over yet, is it?" I asked.

Ignoring my questions, she came within inches of my face, so close I could smell the gin on her breath. "Where the hell is it?" she hissed.

"I don't know what you're talking about," I lied.

"You sure as hell know what I'm talking about. Where's my box? You took it. I know you did, Bertie! Now, where is it?"

"Your what?" I feigned ignorance.

"Don't play dumb with me," she seethed. "You think I'm stupid?"

"No, Mama. I don't think you're stupid, I know you are," I said defiantly.

Mama reacted with the speed of a viper striking its prey, slapping me upside the face with her open palm. "I'll ask again. WHERE THE HELL IS MY BOX?!"

The blow stung, but it didn't begin to match my smoldering hatred for her at that very moment. "Where's the money you stole from me?" I demanded, rubbing my swelling left cheek. "Where's my money, or did you drink it all?" Mama raised her hand to strike again, only this time I reached out and stopped her swing in midair. "If you lay a hand on me again, you'd better sleep every night from here on with one eye open. Which will be difficult for you, considering you fall asleep every night in your gin-soaked dreamland."

Mama bowed her head as if in defeat. She staggered over and collapsed on the bed. "Please, please," she pleaded, "give it back to me. It's mine."

"No," I said, without so much as a smattering of empathy.

"Please, you have no right to take what's mine." She sniffed and wiped away tears from her cheeks.

"You had no right to steal me blind. Now we're even." I turned, stepping toward the door. I wanted to run, but my feet stayed planted in the doorway. The humiliation from Mama's blow stoked the embers of hate deep within my soul and I knew I was still owed my pound of flesh.

"You don't understand," Mama said.

I spun around. "Enlighten me, Mama. What's so important about that box? Why do you keep a dead lightning bug in a jar?"

She looked at me, her eyes crossing a bit, trying to bring me into focus from across the room. It was frightening to see the hatred emanating from the puffy slits on her face. "You don't know nothin," she said. "It ain't a lightnin' bug, it's a firefly."

I laughed at her absurdity. "What the hell's the difference? A lightning bug or a firefly, they're the same damn thing."

She sat on the edge of the bed swaying. I imagine that the room was spinning. "You don' unnerstan,'" she said again, shaking her bowed head. She sobbed into her sleeve, and finally looked up at me. "Lightnin' bugs, well, they're just lightnin' bugs. Nothin' special." She wiped her nose again. "But fireflies, well now, they sound a whole lot prettier, don't they? Regal, dignified almost, don't it? Like poetry. A firefly's lights are the dreams we seek. We can see 'em for just a split second, but then, *poof*, they just disappear, like those dreams." Her eyes were red, but she was no longer crying.

I burst out laughing. I remember looking at her as if I was seeing an alien. Who the hell was this person? Whoever it was, this wasn't my mama. I'd never heard her talk like that. Just outta meanness and after I stopped laughing, I added a little more fuel to the already burning trash fire. "It still doesn't make them anything but lightning bugs, no matter whatcha call 'em."

"Bertie, it's about how you see things."

I was stunned. I folded my arms and shook my head. "You amaze me, Mama. Your vision sure doesn't match this life of yours. When have you *ever* had a dream? You've spent most of your life being such a nightmare."

She just stared at me, too tired to fight any more. "Just gimme back my goddamn box, Bertie," she whispered. And there it was, Glennis Campbell was back. Her next words slapped me harder than her hand across my face. "It's all I have left of him."

I felt rage. "No, it's not, Mama. You seem to forget— he left you me."

I turned and stormed out of her room that day vowing she'd never get this box back. I shake off the bad memories. It's all water under the bridge. One week from today, all this will be history. I'm getting the hell out of this place—far, far away from Mama, and I'm not looking back. I'm not fooling myself, though, I know there'll be parts of this place I'll miss, especially my friends, and Billy. I've often heard Estill County described by folks passing through as a charming place—quaint, picturesque. *Everyone's so friendly around here* is a common phrase. They just don't know the ugliness and secrets hiding behind closed doors, camouflaged by the land's solemn beauty. The sister cities of Irvine and Ravenna have been home to me all my eighteen years. It's all I've known. The biggest thing besides the coal industry and railroad in these parts is Carhartt, the clothing company where many folks from the area work, but Mama got fired last year for being late for the umpteenth time, and that's why she works at the grocery store now, and why we still live in the same old rundown house. As much as I hate my ugly life with Mama, I step outside these four walls and fall in love with what's around me every time. Our two towns are cradled in the arm of the Kentucky River valley, just on the edge of the Cumberland Plateau. The Red River gorge borders us on the north. I heard someone say once that Estill County rocks in the ample bosom of Lady Bluegrass, and it always makes me giggle a bit, glancing down at my own less than impressive cleavage. At times when I'm free to wander, I swear I hear God talking to me. Oh, not literally. I'm not even sure I believe in a God like other people do, mainly cuz I can't imagine that if there's truly a God, why'd he'd go and give me a mama like this. But when I look around, I do believe there must be some sort of higher power and that my vision is the conduit from which it communicates. There are mornings when a moist blue mist blankets our hills, showing reverence like a veiled widow. Winged warriors, large and small, soar the treetops, and only the whispers of Mother Nature can be heard. This I will miss. The spirit of the hills, the majesty of the mountains, my best friends, and of course, my Billy. A tightness grips my chest and I swallow hard, trying to stop the swell of sorrow and guilt forming within me. How can I up and leave, just abandon this sweet, sweet boy? In the end he'll probably hate me, and I'll always love him, but I'll just die if I have to remain here much longer. Don't I deserve my own dreams? I know my heart will undoubtedly ache in the absence of these people, for the beauty of Estill County. But not for Mama.

Present Day

FIVE

When I left the river this afternoon, I came home and sprawled out on my bed. That's where I am now, staring up at the ceiling. I did manage to change into comfy gray sweats, a t-shirt, and my favorite winter-white cardigan. My discarded blouse and skirt are on the floor where I left them in a heap. I'm cold. I sit up, grab a pillow, and hug it tight to my chest, using it as a protective shield. I rest my head against the headboard. This house is cold. I glance at the fireplace and wish the thing was working. I wonder what good it is if it doesn't work. It's gorgeous, though, with the framed mirror and its mantel encased in dark mahogany and adorned with decorative corbels. The exquisite wood carvings of flower petals, flowing vines, leaves, and even shell patterns are etched above and below the monstrous piece. It's almost identical to the fireplaces in the living and dining rooms. Only the fireplaces downstairs work. Well, they did last time I checked, though I don't remember the last time I used any of them. I keep meaning to get someone over here to look at them. I don't know why I'm thinking about fireplaces. Yes, I do. I don't want to think about the other.

I finally get up. My bare feet sink into the plush cream-colored rug. I need socks. I walk to the dresser and retrieve a thick pair, balancing on one foot and then the other as I pull each sock over my frozen appendages. Once my feet are sufficiently clad in warmth, I still don't move. My attention is fixated on the drawer to the left of the dresser. The drawer I've been thinking about and afraid to open since arriving home. What if it's not there? What if someone's taken it? I know there's only one way to find out, so I slowly open the drawer wide enough to see inside. Scarves, slips, camisoles, and hosiery are folded neatly on top. From what I can tell, nothing looks disturbed. With a shaky hand I push the clothes aside, exposing the remnants of an ill-forgotten time capsule of sorts. Like an archeological dig, the tin is in the exact spot it's been since the day I left it there, under layers of my life. Relief and nausea commingle, causing my belly to knot. I lift the small box and it feels strangely warm, like a sleepy child being lifted from the comforting folds of its blanket. I carry the tiny tin to the window seat and place it on the cushion, folding my right leg underneath me as I sit next to the remnants of my youth. Minutes pass, but I don't open it. I just focus on it, anticipating maybe an explosion that will leave the life I know in pieces. I narrow my eyes as I scrutinize its exterior, noting it hasn't changed much through the years. Its finial handle, once painted solid gold, is now rather nebulous and blotched with gold paint flecks. Further examination of the box is disturbed by a familiar *meow*. Simone, my orange tabby, has decided to join me at the windowsill. I'm surprised she wasn't already here curled up on the cushion. The branches of the huge oak tree out front reach all the way to the top of my bedroom window. It's a perfect viewing area for my feline boarder to watch birds and squirrels, nature's ESPN channel for cats. Simone is usually buried deep in a sea of pillows, either in the living room or in my bedroom. I pick her up and try to cuddle her. "Where you been, girl?" She meows again and contorts herself so that she can escape my grasp, leaping to freedom. I named her Simone after the gymnast Simone Biles because of her incredible feats of acrobatic strength. Simone only allows me to show signs of affection on her terms. Maybe that's like most cats. I'm not a cat person, dogs are more my style, but this cat showed up on my front porch a few days before Halloween and wouldn't go away. I talked to neighbors, distributed flyers, and constantly checked the online neighborhood page for missing cats. Nothing. By Thanksgiving, she'd become a permanent resident. I worry if one day, just like me, someone will come knocking on my door looking for her.

Simone makes herself comfortable, and I turn back to the box. I haven't looked at it in a long while. After today's mysterious phone call, I thought quite possibly someone had broken in and taken it, though I know it was irrational to think that. I was still terrified to look and see whether it was still in the drawer, but here it is. And whoever called today knows about it and is either trying to scare me, or maybe warn me.

I finally reach over, pick it up, and put it in my lap. I take a deep breath and open it, halfway expecting something to jump out. Nothing's missing, nothing seems to be disturbed in any way. I take out each object, handling each one as if it's a precious artifact. I line them up on the seat cushion. Everything's there: the bandana, the perfume bottle, the photographs, and the jar containing the firefly. I did add another item to the box years ago, another photograph. This one has that greenish-brown tint to it, like so many taken at that time. I hold it up, gazing at the image of Marie, Audrey, Eve, and me. It was taken with Eve's camera in front of the Good Eats diner, maybe a week or so after we graduated high school. It was serendipitous that we found a rare afternoon to spend time together, when none of us were working or tending to chores at home. Eve was dabbling in photography, so she brought her camera along to practice her latest hobby. I remember it was a warm day, and we'd stopped for ice cream and then just meandered around downtown Irvine. We were standing in front of the diner when this photo was taken. Why, I'm not sure. Marie probably stopped to gossip or tell a dirty joke and at some point one of us must have asked someone to take our picture. It's been too long to remember.

Did we ever really look like that? Marie's face is animated, and she's effervescent, with her head thrown back and laughter on her lips. She herself *is* a picture, framed in a tight crown of curls lassoed by a brightly colored scarf. Her pretty elfin face is shining. She's wearing a halter top and skin-tight shorts that barely cover her ass. She looks almost as tall as Audrey with the platform sandals she's wearing. Looking at her now, she reminds me of Jody Foster in *Taxi*. She's got one hand in the pocket of her shorts and the other's holding an ice cream cone. Marie simply screams *sex*.

Then there's Audrey. Her thick mane of auburn tresses puddle around her shoulders in waves. I always envied her hair. Her skin is fair, and though they can't be seen in the photograph, freckles lightly populate her nose and cheeks. Her tall, slim body is clad in a dark tank top and her long limbs are encased in tight, hip-hugger bell-bottoms. She's the tallest of us, maybe around five eight, if I remember right. She's gazing up at the sky, eyes squinting a bit from the sun, lips partially open, with barely a hint of a smile. Audrey was our Mona Lisa, my best friend...serious, somber Audrey.

Next to Audrey stands Eve, almost a dwarf by comparison. Eve's ordinary appearance doesn't match her extraordinary talent, possessing a fantastical aura that dwells within her small frame. She's a wisp of a girl. Her thin brown hair is cut just below her ears. I guess it would be called a bob. She's wearing a striped fitted shirt with sleeves about two inches above the elbow, tucked into bell-bottom jeans. A macramé belt, most definitely made by her own hands, completes the outfit. She's smiling, but in a shy way, her ice cream melting. Poor Eve, I think. Poor sweet, awkward, extraordinary Eve.

Then there's me. I hardly recognize the girl I was. My hair's almost black. It's parted in the middle and hangs down the sides of my face in thick waves past my waist. Audrey's just a couple inches taller than me, but I've got a long torso that makes me appear taller than I am. Kids at school used to laugh and call me Cher. Mama never allowed me to cut my hair because Cher was Mama's favorite singer. Just thinking about Mama triggers hostility deep within me. I shove those feeling aside and look back at the picture. I'm wearing a gauzy, white tunic blouse over a pair of cut-offs and sneakers. I remember that blouse, though. It was one of the first things I bought with my own money. I loved it. I'm also grinning in the photo, as if I just got the joke. There we stand, innocently laughing and eating ice cream, unaware that in just a few short weeks, our lives would be forever changed.

I put down the photo and pick up the jar containing the firefly. I hold it up to the light, looking at it from all angles, locked forever in its glass tomb. Even now I still feel angry. I'm tempted to get up and flush it down the toilet, but I know I won't. I open the perfume bottle, inhaling. It smells strangely of roses and wood sage. It triggers something familiar, but I can't quite place it. I put the bottle back in the box and pick up the other photos. I look at Glennis and Jesse Campbell and wonder if these two ever loved each other the way Joe and I did. My eyes fill with tears just thinking about Joe. *Oh God, how I miss him.* If he were here right now, he'd be holding me, stroking my hair, and telling me everything's gonna be alright. He's the only person I ever shared my past with.

Simone decides at that moment to hop in my lap. See? Like I said, always her terms. I stroke her silky coat, she arches her back and stretches as if to say to me in cat language, *Awww, that's the spot*. After I've given her the massage she's demanded, I set her on the floor, gather up the items, place them back in the box, and return it to its resting place. I don't consider it a hiding place, because I've never really kept it hidden. One day, when Annie was about ten years old, I found her on the floor of my bedroom, the box open, the things out.

She looked scared at first because she'd been caught. I stood in the doorway with my arms crossed and a smile on my face. "Whatcha doin'?"

She looked a bit guilty. "Mom, I found this can in your drawer. What are these things?"

I wasn't angry, she was just doing what kids do, rooting through stuff, being curious. I told her, "They're memories of people and things from my past. People that are now no longer in my life and the things associated with them. They're pieces of 'not so good' memories. Remember, I told you I didn't come from a very happy place. I guess I keep them because they'll always be part of me. I keep them tucked away to remind me of how lucky I am now. How lucky I am your father loved me and gave me you. Maybe when you're older, I'll explain more." That seemed to satisfy her. We've never spoken of it since.

I suddenly feel faint and realize I haven't eaten all day. I go downstairs and search the fridge. I haven't done much shopping for a while, but I do have some tuna salad that's still fresh. I smell it though, just to be sure. Seems okay. Besides, if I die of food poisoning, my problems will be over. I chance it, taking the container out of the fridge, along with some strawberries, purple grapes, and a wedge of cheddar cheese. This oughta do the trick. I scour the cabinets for some crackers and am in luck. I find half a sleeve of saltines and add them to the menu. I go back to the refrigerator and grab a half bottle of Kendall Jackson Chardonnay. I stop. Maybe not such a good idea on an empty stomach. I put it back and decide on water for now. I carry my meager dinner into the living room. Soft evening light streams in from the bay window. It's been staying light a tad later now that spring's finally arrived. Thank God. I think I'm one of those people who suffer from sun deprivation. Without those solar rays, my mood can shift, and not in a good way. I look around this comfortable room. I always feel grounded here. It strangely settles me, mostly because of the light that filters in, its cream walls and ten-foot ceilings. I feel like I can breathe. The dark woodwork, the brilliant staircase, and the handcrafted fireplace give the place so much character. I've decorated this old place in mostly neutrals, but there are splashes of color everywhere. Throw pillows in shades of aqua, yellow, and even vibrant red. I have lots of live plants and beautiful artwork—sculptures, pottery, and paintings, mostly collected by Joe and me in the early years. This is my happy place. I set the tray on the coffee table and hear Simone behind me. "Crap, I forgot your dinner, didn't I?" I stuff a cracker in my mouth to keep myself from fainting and head back to the kitchen to feed her. I sure as hell know that if I don't do it now, I won't be allowed to eat in peace. I quickly open a can of Fancy Feast and check her water bowl. She saunters over and dismisses me with a meow. "You know, this is my house?" I say. She ignores me.

I find the remote and turn on the television. The local news will be on shortly, and I'm sure the trial will be mentioned. After shoving several bites into my mouth, the food finally reaches my stomach and I begin to feel better. The lightheadedness dissipates. The meal's almost finished when I see a familiar face on the screen—me. I quickly turn up the volume and listen to myself answer the reporter's questions from this morning. I look like the wrath of God and sullen. Not the face of an attorney who's just won the case for her client. My hair is wild and crazy, like Medusa's, and I wish I'd fastened it earlier that morning before going to court.

The next footage is of Jack Hamilton. I guess if I were being honest with myself, I can understand what Annie sees in him. He's extremely handsome, confident, and a successful prosecutor for a young man of maybe thirty-seven, thirty-eight, somewhere around there. But I've always been leery of people who appear just a little too perfect.

"What's your reaction to today's verdict?" asks the female reporter for WHAS.

"Well, of course we're disappointed. We wanted justice for the Bauer family, and justice wasn't served today," Jack says.

"Why do you think the jury returned a verdict of not guilty?"

Jack smiles, flashing that brilliant set of teeth. "Well, we have to take some responsibility for that. It was up to the prosecution to establish burden of proof, and in this case, we failed—I failed—to do that."

"Thank you," says the reporter. "Well, there you have it. Emma Davies was found not guilty by a jury of her peers and tonight is a free woman. I'm Jennifer Mitchell, WHAS 11."

The news turns to the weather, and I watch briefly just to see if my friend the sun will be making any appearances the rest of the week. It's not altogether promising, so I turn it off, carry my dishes to the sink, and rinse them before placing them in the dishwasher. I glance out the window. The view from the sink isn't great, just the red brick from Rita Hollinger's house next door. She's a widow too, but in her seventies, I would think. I dry my hands and walk to the back door of the kitchen, checking to make sure everything's still locked up tight. I gaze out the back. It's almost dusk now. My tiny backyard could use an entire makeover. The metal café table and two chairs are in the center of the yard. A very sad-looking citronella candle sits on the table and hasn't been moved since this past summer. A row of low-growing shrubs, mostly bare branches, and an old wood fence separate my yard from the back of the brick building that houses the bookstore. The backyard's been on my list of things to do for a long time. I sigh and wonder if I'll ever get to that either. My train of thought is interrupted by the doorbell.

Who could it possibly be? I'm not expecting anyone. My heart is beating fast. I slowly creep down the hall, fearful of being heard. I stand there, holding my breath, trying not to move. The doorbell rings again, followed by a loud knock. I hear the words, "Mom, are you there? It's me."

I'm flooded with relief. I release the air I've been holding in my lungs, and yell, "I'm coming," before opening the door and letting Annie in.

"Mom, are you okay? I've been calling and calling. Why haven't you answered your phone?"

"Oh, my gosh, darling, I'm so sorry. I came home and laid down. I took your advice and got a bit of rest. When I finally made my way back downstairs, I must have left my phone upstairs. I didn't realize I didn't have it with me. I certainly didn't mean to scare you."

"Well, I am scared, Mom. When I got back to the office, Beaker told me you left in a hurry after he gave you a message about a phone call. What's going on?"

"Nothing really, Annie, nothing. Everything's fine. I was just tired from the trial. You can understand that."

"Yes, I can, but I don't think you're telling me the truth," she challenges.

For a split second, I see Glennis Campbell's face in my daughter and go weak in the knees. For everything I love about Annie, the fact that she's the spitting image of her grandmother, especially when she becomes angry or scared, totally unnerves me. I feel like I'm about to fall.

Annie quickly sees that I'm a bit unsteady. "Mom, come sit down." She guides me to the couch. "You've got to tell me what's going on. Please, you can tell me anything, you know that. Are you sick? Is someone threatening you? Are you in trouble? Please, talk to me."

I study my daughter's beautiful face and don't know how or where to begin. Even if I could find a place to start the narrative, I'm not ready to share my story with Annie or anyone else right now. Not yet. I choose my words carefully. "Annie, you're not wrong. There is something going on. And believe me when I say I want nothing more than to share it with you. But I can't, not just yet. I promise, though, in time, I will tell you everything."

"Now you're really scaring me, Mom..."

"Try not to be scared. I assure you, I'm in no physical harm, you're in no physical harm, it's nothing like that. It's just something that I must resolve. Everything's going to be fine. I promise you. You're going to have to trust me."

Finally, she says, "Okay. I do trust you."

"Thank you. I love you!"

"Me too." She pauses then adds, "This is probably a lousy time to tell you this then."

"Tell me what?" I say, not sure I can handle anything more tonight.

"Well, I wasn't completely honest with you when I told you I was having lunch with Jack this afternoon."

"No? Then what?"

"We didn't go to lunch. Jack went with me to the doctor's office. It looks like he and I are going to have a baby. You're going to be a grandmother."

I gasp. My mouth opens, but no words come out.

"Well, aren't you going to say anything?"

I grab her, wrapping my arms around her. I really can't speak. I'm overwhelmed, jubilated, but at the same time terrified I may not be a part of this child's life.

"Oh honey, I'm so happy for you! And Jack? How's he taking the news?"

"He's thrilled, he really is. He's being very supportive and we're going to take our time deciding things. I know how you feel about him, but I do believe I love him, and now with the baby, he's going to be very much a part of our lives, whether you like it or not."

"Oh, honey, this isn't about how I feel. It's about how you and Jack feel about each other."

"He says he loves me. I want to believe it. Right now, I'm—we're—going to take it one day at a time."

"Then I'll take one day at a time with you. You're going to make a wonderful mother, honey."

"Can you believe it, though? I'm going to have a baby. We're debating on finding out the sex early, but we'll see."

"Well, you're only surprised once," I say, laughing.

When we're talked out, she heads home. I'm completely wiped, physically and mentally drained and unable to think straight. It's time for me to call it a day. I check the locks, set the alarm, and turn out the lights. I manage to find the strength to pull my nightgown over my head, but just barely. Everything feels like an effort. I go in the bathroom to wash my face and brush my teeth, gazing at my reflection in the clouded mirror. Like me, the glass is affected by time, all the years have taken their toll. I can barely recognize the face in the mirror anymore. My hair, usually my best feature, resembles a bird's nest. Frown lines crease my forehead. I pull my hair back with my hand and squint, narrowing my eyes to really look. All that does is cause more frown lines. *Maybe it's time for some bangs,* I think. *Oh, hell, what does it matter now anyway? Like bangs are going to solve my problems.* The time for vanity is long past.

I turn out the light and crawl into bed. Though I'm exhausted, I have a feeling it's going to take me awhile to find sleep. Thoughts are swirling in my head. They begin with Annie, move to the baby, and then to Joe. Before long, my thoughts turn darker, slipping into another time and place. A time in my life when all I had was Marie, Audrey, Eve, and of course, last and always least, Mama.

1975

SIX

Estill County, Kentucky

"Mama, I'm heading out," I call from the bottom of the stairs. "Mama, do you hear me?" Of course she doesn't hear me. I'll bet she's too hung over to lift her head off the pillow. I heard her come in late last night, knocking over the lamp that's now lying on the floor in the foyer. The shade is cracked and bent. Miraculously, the naked bulb isn't shattered and is still glowing. Mama never even picked it up. It's a wonder she didn't burn the entire house down with us in it. From the sounds of her entrance, she could barely keep herself upright. The few framed pictures that are hanging on the wall leading up the staircase are cockeyed. All I can do is shake my head. Just another day in the Campbell house. I pick up the lamp, straighten the damaged shade, and place it back where it belongs. The circular outline of dust on the foyer table marks its spot. This lamp must be a thousand years old, fossilized, and that's probably why it didn't break. That lamp is just like Mama—it's old, it's seen better days, but by some miracle, it's still working.

I hate her. She hates me. I hate my father for leaving us in this mess. I hate Mama more. I hate my life. But that's going to change.

I make a final check before leaving. I'm wearing my blue waitressing uniform, with its wide white collar and button-down shirtdress tapered at the waist. I only have two uniforms, which I alternate between washings. I've had the same two since I started at the diner, back when I was a sophomore in high school. They're both a bit tight now, but the men sure don't complain. I'm carrying my old quilted bag with my change of clothes. I take one more look inside to make sure I have what I need: bugspray, matches, a flashlight, my favorite peasant blouse, a pair of cutoffs, and my sneakers. Yep, everything's there. I'm not coming back to the house tonight. Audrey and I are hooking up with Eve and Marie and heading to our secret place down by the river. We have a special spot no one else knows about. Well, I'm sure we're not the only ones who know about it, but we like to think it's our special place. We've been meeting there for as long as we've known each other. Marie led us to the spot the night we snuck out of the church lock-in. We've been using it ever since, whenever we want a place to get away. It's what's left of an old, abandoned shed close to the river's edge. The night of Eve's crucifixion, Marie exposed us to a whole new world. She'd been coming to that place for a while—a place to take advantage of her contraband corn liquor and cigarettes she kept then. They're in a secure place, a large, rusty old pipe, hidden in a wall of the shack. We didn't feel too great the next morning, but boy did we have a good time at our own little lock-in. From then on, when we could, we'd bring blankets, build a fire, drink, smoke, laugh, and listen to the radio when reception was good. We could all use a little fun right now. Just us girls. Of course, Marie's bringing the booze (she's on a first-name basis with all the bootleggers in Estill County). Eve's bringing the new radio she got for her eighteenth birthday last month. Audrey and I are making sandwiches before we leave work. We're looking forward to an evening without boys or suffocating parents. Since it's a Friday night, most of our friends will be out cruising the Starlight—the most popular spot on the weekends. We're usually right there with them, circling the restaurant in Audrey's car, waiting for someone to pull out so we can take their spot. At the Starlight, you can buy a cheeseburger, fries, and a shake for a little more than a dollar. It's the place to go when you're young in Estill County. Kids hanging out of car windows, whooping and hollering, radios tuned to the Lexington or Richmond stations, blaring songs like "Black Water" by the Doobie Brothers or "Get Down Tonight" by KC and the Sunshine Band, or Elvis or Mac Davis. You can usually hear a little bit of everything over the souped-up mufflers—boys displaying pseudo-masculinity by gunning their engines. But tonight, tonight, we've decided that we just need some girl time. Besides, I want to tell Marie and Eve about my plan. I've already told Audrey, and it was painful seeing the look on her face, not that she isn't happy for me, but because she hates to see me go.

I'm so glad Marie can come with us tonight, and she doesn't have to spend it with that Neanderthal of a boyfriend. Most the time she's never out of Eddy's sight. Marie's dealing with a guy who knocks her around for sport. We've been trying to get her to leave that son-of-a-bitch for a long time, but she's either blind to the fact that he's not going to change or she's just in a state of denial. She keeps making excuses for him, like I used to do with people when it came to Mama and her out-of-control behavior. Marie tells us he doesn't really mean it when he tells her to shut her mouth. "He's just got a bit of a temper," she'll say, even after he's left bruises from shoving her around. I've seen her with a black eye on more than one occasion. She continuously gives him a pass. "He just gets frustrated. He's under so much pressure," she says. We all know it's bullshit because Eddy Dennison is just plain evil, and she's not fooling any of us with her false justifications. I think it would have been different if Marie's older brother Warren were still around—he was her protector and wouldn't have let Eddy lay a finger on her. But he was killed in Vietnam the year before last and Marie's never gotten over it. Now she's got nobody to protect her against this complete *dick*. I've warned Marie more than once to drop him before he does something that might land her in the hospital. She says she's not worried, and besides, he'll be heading to the University of Kentucky this fall on a football scholarship. He switched from basketball to football freshman year when his height, or lack thereof, was no longer an advantage on the court and the rest of his body seemed to thicken up. I will give him some credit; he has a natural athletic ability on the field, and he's the football hero of the county. His daddy's a big muckety-muck in the coal business and folks around here turn a blind eye. Eddy can get by with just about anything except back-talking his daddy. Folks 'round here say there's splinters of cruelty that run deep in the Dennison family. Marie's biding her time. Once he goes off to college, she says she'll be free of him. He'll find himself another girl—or several others—to knock around. She says she's not worried, that he's exciting to be around, even if he is a little dangerous, and maybe it's *because* he's a little dangerous. Marie doesn't do boring. So, in the meantime, until she finds greener pastures, she's still with him. He can't leave fast enough, in my opinion. I never told Marie that last year he cornered me back behind the diner. I was taking out the trash when he came outta nowhere. Completely took me off guard.

He grabbed me, told me how pretty I was and smart, that he always wanted a "piece" of me. When he tried to kiss me, I bit his lip and delivered a knee to his groin. For just a split second, I was able to escape back into the diner, locking the door behind me. Thank God Jimmy, our cook, was still there. Nobody messes with Jimmy—he's about six-foot-five with a well-fed frame. But Eddy, he's mean, and I know down deep inside that Marie's been around Eddy long enough to be scared of him; she just feels trapped right now. She lied and told Eddy her daddy grounded her tonight so she could have a free night with us. I just pray he doesn't find out.

Then there's Eve. The only child of Mildred and Donald Henderson. They own the Henderson Hardware Store in Irvine but live in Ravenna. Mildred Henderson was forty-nine when she discovered she was pregnant. She'd been told by doctors she was barren. According to Eve, they'd given up on having a family, so imagine the shock at discovering that they were to become first-time parents at their age. Eve always says they gave birth to their own grandchild. We would laugh when she'd say it, but it's really not funny, it's almost as if they stole her youth at birth, if that makes any sense. Her parents are extremely protective. Eve's a serious, creative, almost haunting soul—maybe it's because she has aging parents. But I think it's more than that, I think it's the extraordinary gift she's been blessed with. Eve's an artist, a writer, a jewel. Strange, beautiful Eve dreams of going to New York City and becoming a famous painter, or maybe a writer. She has a talent like no one else in Ravenna. Heck, maybe not even in the state of Kentucky, or in the U.S. for that matter. Eve's mother said that at three years old, Eve could draw any animal you asked her to. In high school, Eve won every art or writing contest she ever competed in. It's not unusual for people in town to ask her to paint or draw pictures of their family members for their birthday or holidays to give them as gifts. She's always writing stories and sharing them with only us, in our secret place. We love them. People think she's strange, and well, she is, but it's because they don't understand her. She looks at things differently. I guess through an artist's lens. She's quiet, imaginative, introspective... and she almost scares me with her intensity. Eve's like an exotic creature who is trapped in the confines of the Kentucky valley. Her parents have other plans for her, which don't include Greenwich Village or SoHo, or any other place she dreams of making her escape. She won't go though, for all her God-given talents, loyalty to her parents exceeds her own ambitions and that's the saddest part of all.

I pick up the pace in order to get to the diner on time. I'm glad Audrey's working today. I got her the waitressing job at the diner last year, and we always have a couple night shifts together, as well as Saturdays. The diner's closed on Sundays for obvious reasons. People in these parts are expected to attend church in the mornings, and for the real dedicated flock, evening services. Any other part of the day is to be spent with the family. Stores are closed, everything's shut down on the sabbath, with the exception of all the church ministers dispensing their godly advice through sermons, warning us sinners that we will surely pay a price for our evil deeds if repentance isn't shown through attendance and tithing on Sundays.

I look at my watch and realize I've got five minutes to get to the diner. I promised Mr. Mason that I'd get here early to open up. Mr. Mason's taking Mrs. Mason to the doctor, and I think it might be serious, but he hasn't said anything. It's just a feeling I have. I hope everything's alright. The Masons have been awfully good to me and I'm going to miss them when I'm gone. They've been about as close to me as anyone I've ever known, besides the girls. They understand my circumstances and have always been there, whether it's an extra meal or sometimes a place to stay if things have gotten really bad with Mama. I don't think I woulda even had a Christmas present if it weren't for Mrs. Mason knitting me a scarf and a pair of mittens. My last two Christmas meals have been spent right here at the diner with the Masons. I remember last year Mrs. Mason fixed me up some turkey, dressing, and gravy to take home for Mama, so that she might have Christmas dinner. I spent Christmas night cleaning turkey, dressing, and gravy off the kitchen walls. Luckily, I dodged the flying leftovers. Mama didn't appreciate the handout, and she made that very clear. Still, I owe the Masons a debt of gratitude for the kindness they've shown me these past few years. I'll probably never be able to repay them.

Though it's early, the sun's up and the heat's already making its presence felt. Perspiration clings to my collar. Not surprising, it's July. I reach the diner and enter through the back door as I always do, tossing my bag in the back room and begin preparing for the day, making coffee and getting supplies out for Jimmy. He should be here soon to prepare for the breakfast crowd. I start the coffee.

I'm raising the shades in the front of the diner when I hear the back door open.

"Hello, beautiful!" Jimmy bellows from the back.

"Hiya, Jimmy, how you doin' today?" I call out.

"I'm alive and that makes it a good day." His response on any given day.

I walk back to greet him. "How can I help you this morning?" I throw the dishcloth over my shoulder, my hands on my hips.

"Why don't you get me a couple dozen eggs from the cooler and a pound a bacon fer starters, beautiful? Oh yeah, that coffee sure does smell good. Would ya mind bringing a cup of that back here for me, darlin'?" He winks as he drapes the apron over his head, tying it in the back.

"You got it."

Jimmy King's the kindest man I know, though he looks a little rough around the edges with his large intimidating frame. But he's really a gentle giant, unless, well, I wouldn't want to piss him off. He's missing more teeth than what's left in his head, but he's been Mr. Mason's cook for as long as I can remember. He's got a bit of a past, but before he landed in Irvine, no one really knows where he came from, except south, the direction he was coming from when he was riding the rails. He wears what looks like some sort of homemade tattoo in the shape of a lion on his right arm. It could indicate some prison time. Nobody really knows that, either, or I doubt anybody has the nerve to ask. What we do know is what Jimmy himself has shared with us. He'd been traveling by train, not in the conventional way, but by hitchin' a ride without an invitation, if you know what I mean. He tells the story that when the train made a stop in Irvine, he was almost caught sleepin' in one of the boxcars. He managed to wrangle up his few belongings as quick as a flash and leave before they threw him off. Being hungry and all, he wandered into town and stood outside the diner staring through the window. Mr. Mason, being the kind person he is, motioned for him to come around back. Mr. Mason proceeded to feed him and even let him sleep in the back room of the diner for the night. Jimmy says Mrs. Mason was mad as a hornet and wasn't all too pleased with her husband for extending that invitation to a hobo. But, come the next morning, Mr. Mason found ol' Jimmy up with the crows, frying up eggs, bacon, and hash browns. That was the morning Mr. Mason stopped cooking and Jimmy became the new cook of the Good Eats. Today, his buttermilk biscuits and fluffy pancakes'll make you cry. Jimmy now has his own place, a single room he rents above Mr.

Gregory's garage. He says that's all he needs. Sure beats a boxcar, I bet.

I'm filling up the ketchup bottles when Audrey comes in.

"Hey, there," I say, missing the mouth of the bottle and feeding the counter.

"Hey," she flatly replies.

"Everything okay?" I ask.

"Yeah, fine."

"Why don't I believe you?"

"Really, Bertie, I'm fine." She's irritated.

"No, you're not fine. C'mon, Audrey, it's me. You don't look so good. Do you feel okay?"

"I'll be okay, really, just got a headache."

"You want me to call and see if Helen maybe can take your shift?" Helen's one of our older waitresses. She usually works the dinner hour, but she's always willing to pick up a few extra shifts. "You really look like shit, Audrey. Sorry to say it, but you do."

"Well, gee, thanks for the compliment. But, no, really, I'll be okay. I'll just go in the back and see if there's a bottle of aspirin anywhere."

"Okay, but if you get to feeling worse, you need to go." I finish filling the bottles and clean off the counter. The first of the morning customers are coming through the door, and I don't have time to say anything more about it. I plaster a smile on my face to greet them and begin the day. By mid-afternoon, Audrey and I are tired and smell of grease and coffee, we need a break and finally steal a few precious minutes to grab a Coke and sit. Fridays are always busy, but by this time, patrons are sparse, and it will be a while before the dinner crowd arrives. There are only a few of the regulars seated at the booths, drinking coffee, and talking about God knows what—the weather, the farm prices, their bursitis. I look over at Audrey, cross my eyes, and stick out my tongue, putting a finger to my head and pretending to pull the trigger in a lame attempt to get her to laugh, or at least smile. I get neither a chuckle nor a grin. She still looks ill, but I can't get her to go home and lie down.

"Your head feel any better?" I ask.

"Yeah, it does."

I don't believe her. "Hey, listen, if you're not up for tonight, it's okay. We'll understand."

"No, no, I want to come. I gotta get away from that house. Chiggers and heat are still better than a houseful of men who continuously fart and burp and act like they can't do a thing for themselves. Daddy promised me I could have some time for myself tonight, and that's exactly what I intend to do."

"Okay." She's not totally convincing me.

"How's Billy? Have ya told him yet you're leavin'?" Audrey asks in a hush.

I feel the hard pinch of guilt. "He's good and no, not yet. I just haven't found the right time. He's been working hard at the farm this summer and neither one of us have been able to make much time for each other. I'm sure we'll get together sometime over the weekend."

"I think you're running out of time." Audrey's stating the obvious.

"Hey darlin', can I get some more coffee?" asks Ernest Rader, a friendly old man who's a common fixture around here. Ernest always sits in the corner booth if it's available. We try and keep it open for him. It's the little things.

"I got it, you sit," I say to Audrey. I grab the pot. "Sure thing, Mr. Rader. Is there anything else I can get you? Maybe another piece of that pecan pie?"

"No darlin,' I'd love another one, just like I'd love to take a spin with a young thing like you, but at my age, I know my limits."

"You best not let Mrs. Rader hear you say things like that. You just might find yourself in a heap of trouble," I say with a laugh.

"Well, I *purt' neer* stay in trouble with the Missus. But I'll let you in on a little secret," he says in a conspiratorial tone. Using his index finger, he gestures for me to move in closer. "I might be old, but I can still outrun her, even with this bum knee," he says cackling, then coughing, then hacking severely.

I'm afraid he's about to cough up half a lung, so I hand him his water glass. "Oh, Mr. Rader," I say shaking my head. "You'll never change, will ya?" The bell rings above the door. I look around to see Eddy Dennison standing there, looking mad as a raging bull, nostrils flaring. He's wearing a sleeveless undershirt, which is commonly referred to by our little group as a wife-beater shirt, tucked into jeans. It's appropriate attire for the town bully and the king of vanity. Eddy does everything he can to show off his physique. His hair is long in the front, flopping down over his eyes, which he's constantly having to brush out of the way with his hands or a nod of his head. I have a cure for that. *Cut your hair, idiot,* I think to myself. I'm still holding a half-full pot of coffee and by the looks of Eddy's demeanor, it's in my best interest to hang onto it for a bit.

"Hello, Eddy, if you'd like, you can take a seat anywhere, and I'll be back right back with a menu," I say, putting as much distance as I can between us as I head for the counter.

"I don't want no damn menu."

"Oh, okay then, you already know what you want?"

"Cut the shit, Bertie. Where's Marie?"

"Marie, well I don't have the slightest idea," I say. "As you can see, Eddy, I'm working. How would I know where she is?"

"Cause you bitches know everything about each other, that's why. You girls can't take a piss without telling each other, so I know you're lying. Now, where the hell is she?" Stone-faced and eyes blazing, he looks like he just might combust.

I'm used to rage being flung my way. I'm not afraid of this piece of garbage. Does he really think he can intimidate me? Why, I'd scratch his eyes out if he ever laid a hand on me again. "Like I told you, I don't know where she is. If you're not here to eat, you need to leave."

Without so much as moving his head, his eyes find their next target, and he's now turning his attention to Audrey. "How about you, bitch, you know where she is? Hey, bitch, I'm talking to you, you deaf or somethin'?" He takes a step toward her.

Audrey's now up out of her seat, her face completely colorless. I grip the coffee pot tighter and block his path. "Leave her alone. She doesn't know where Marie is either."

He ignores me. "C'mon, red, where is she? You know." He looks her up and down seductively. "Hey, I've always wanted to know, cunt, does that pussy of yours match the top of that no-brain head of yours?" He's wearing a sickening smile.

Audrey steps around me. "I don't know where she is, but I can guarantee you one thing, if I did, I wouldn't tell you, you piece of shit!" she spat.

I'm not sure which one of us was more shocked, me or Eddy. Audrey's never been confrontational and to take on the biggest bully in the county, well, my God, that takes guts, or stupidity. She just made an enemy of Eddy Dennison, and though he's as dumb as a box of crackers in my opinion, he does have a memory for those who stand up to him.

"You fucking bitch!" he says, charging at her.

Out of nowhere, Jimmy appears, grabbing Eddy by the back of his shirt, spinning him around, and pulling him forward. Eddy's face is now just inches from Jimmy's, and his feet are literally off the ground. "You lay one hand on either one of these fine ladies, and you'll live to regret it," Jimmy says with such conviction that there isn't one of us who at that very moment doesn't believe him.

"Yeah, you think some dumbass, toothless drifter like you's gonna tell me what to do?" Eddy challenges with false bravado.

"Yeah, I think so. It's best you get on outta here, NOW!" Jimmy's raising his voice and giving Eddy a hard shove.

"Fuck you! Fuck all y'all! You better watch your backs," he threatens, practically breaking glass as he storms out.

"Audrey, you okay?" I ask. Her hand covers her mouth, and she bolts to the back of the diner. The coffee pot's still in my hand as the men in the corner booth stare at me in stunned silence. "Hey, guys, will you excuse me for just a moment?" They simply nod yes.

I put down the pot and go find Audrey. She's in the bathroom with the door closed, but there's no mistaking what's happening, I can hear the heaving and gagging from behind the door. I knock softly. "Audrey, it's me, can I come in?" I wait a moment. "Audrey, honey, it's okay, let me in."

"It's open," she whispers.

She's sitting next to the toilet, her head resting against the wall. I grab a paper towel and wet it under the sink. "Oh, sweetie, I'm so sorry. He's such a prick." I wipe her mouth and face with the wet towel. "I gotta say, though, you certainly gave them gentlemen out there a show." I'm trying an attempt at humor to get her to smile. "I don't think they've seen that much action since the war." My comic relief works only slightly. She smiles, but it's a sad smile. "Aww, Audrey, it's alright, you're gonna be alright."

With that, she bursts into tears, shaking her head violently. "*NO! NO! NO!* I'm not gonna be alright! I'm not. I'm never gonna be alright!"

"Of course you are." I put my arm around her. "This'll pass. Eddy blows up and lives to terrorize other defenseless victims of Estill County for another day."

She takes the wet towel from me and wipes her eyes. She finally says, "This isn't about Eddy, Bertie. This is about me. I'm pregnant."

It takes me a minute to register what I've just heard. "I'm sorry, what did you say?"

"You heard me, I'm pregnant."

"Oh God, Audrey, I'm so sorry, I... I... I... who, when? What the hell, Audrey? I didn't even know you were seeing somebody." This time the cry that escapes her sounds more like the torturous wail of a wounded animal.

In all the years I've known Audrey, I've seen her cry maybe twice, when her dog Ditch died and, of course, her mother. Audrey just doesn't get emotional. It's not in her DNA. She's a rock. At least she's been mine.

"Oh God, Audrey, come here, come here." Wrapping her in my arms, I rock her, the front of my uniform wet from her tears. I don't know what else to do and I can't even imagine how frightened she must be. I let her sob in my arms, rocking her as if she herself were a newborn babe. The sobs subside and morph into short staccato breaths, followed by slow deep breaths.

"Here, lean over here," I say, moving her away from the toilet. "Wait here, I'm going to get you some water and tell Jimmy to hold down the fort." In a flash, I'm back and hand her a glass half full. I don't say a word. I don't know what to say. She looks like a ragdoll leaning against the wall with her legs splayed out in front, her head slightly tilted to the side. "Drink," I say. She sips. After a minute or so, I gently ask, "Do you want to talk about it?"

"No, no I don't." A full minute goes by as we sit on the floor in silence until she breaks it. "No, I don't want to tell anybody, but I gotta, before I die inside. Keeping it to myself is killing me. But you gotta swear to me, Bertie, I mean really swear to me, you won't tell a soul, no matter what. Do you swear? I gotta hear you swear?" She pleads, her nails damn near piercing my skin.

"I swear, Audrey. I swear. You're my best friend. I promise I won't say a word. Your secret's safe with me." I wait a moment, but she's not saying anything. "So?"

"The fa....," she chokes up. She tries again. "The baby's father..., well, it's my daddy." My mind explodes, right then and there. I can't even respond. "After Mama died, he started coming to my room at night. I thought he'd stop eventually cause he was just lonely, and you know, I thought maybe he'd find himself a lady friend and then he'd stop. But he never stopped, Bertie, he never stopped. I asked him to, I really did." She starts crying again, but this time they are silent tears, and it's as if she's holding the weight of the world inside. She's angrily wiping her tears away with the palms of both hands. "You know what he said to me the last time he climbed off me? He tol' me I might as well quit them tears cause it's time for me to grow up."

The anguish on her face is more than I can bear. She's broken, and I don't know how to fix her. I don't know what to do. "Oh, Audrey, I'm so, so sorry. I didn't know. Oh, honey. Oh, you poor, poor thing. I didn't know. That monster, that, that, oh God! He's gotta pay for this. He can't get away with this. You gotta tell someone, Audrey! He should be locked up for this!"

"NO, THAT'S EXACTLY WHAT I DON'T WANT!" she said in sheer terror. "I should have never told you!"

"No, you were right to tell me. It's okay, I get it, calm down. We'll figure this out, I promise. Together, we'll figure this out. You're not alone. You got me, you got Marie, you got Eve. We're here for you."

"How you gonna help me, Bertie? You'll be gone in a week."

I search her face, realizing what she's saying is true, and that she's absolutely right. I don't respond right away, giving myself time to think. Then, in that moment, as if the clouds part and the sun comes shining through, I have the answer. "No," I say, "we'll be gone in a week, cause your comin' with me. He's not going to hurt you anymore." And I mean every word of it.

Present Day

SEVEN

I wake up to Lizzo singing "Good as Hell." As much as I love that song, I fumble for the off switch on my clock radio, failing on several attempts until finally making contact. Silence. *Thank God!* I'm not ready to get up, so I pull the covers up over my head, attempting to shut out the world, if only for a few minutes longer. I play dead for another half hour before giving in. I drag myself to a sitting position, sweeping the hair from my eyes, giving my vision a chance to focus. When I'm a little more awake, I reach for the phone on my bedside table to check for messages and emails. There's only a couple of messages that are work-related and no anticipated email. I really don't get it. Why haven't I been contacted yet? Why the phone call to the office leaving a cryptic message, why not just send another email with a time and place? I swear, I think somebody's screwing with me. They've got to be. It just doesn't make sense. Well, hell, none of it ever made sense. It's hard for me to face the fact that I even had another life before coming to Louisville. For me, I wasn't even born until I arrived here. It was a rebirth, a new beginning, a starting over and never, ever, fucking *ever* looking back. When you tell yourself that, when you fucking spend years making yourself believe it, well, you find the strength to make it through another day, and then another, and another. It's another day. I get up.

I jump in the shower and quickly dress, taking no time to ready myself for whatever shitshow I might be facing today. I want to get into the office and do something that even remotely appears to resemble a normal workday. If I could just have five minutes without being invaded by my own paranoid thoughts of an apocalyptic end of the world for me.

I enter the kitchen and Simone's sitting in front of her food bowl, tail swishing. I guess it's her version of what humans do when drumming their fingers, letting me know that she's waiting and not pleased about it.

"I'm coming, I'm coming. Hold your horses," I say to her.

She responds with a rather lengthy *meoooowwww*.

I brew a quick cup of coffee, fill her food and water bowls, and watch her eat breakfast as I sip my first cup of the day. I'm feeling a bit better and decide I'll grab some food at the diner before work. Perhaps by then I'll have an appetite, but the thought of eating right now makes me queasy.

"Goodbye, Simone, you have a good day," I say as I rinse out my coffee cup and lay it in the sink. Simone simply looks up as if to say, *Oh, you're still here.* She proceeds to lick her paws. I am dismissed.

I reach the office, and I'm the first one here. I turn on the lights and fire up my computer, wasting no time catching up on some emails and preparing for anything new that might be coming up. I have a few court appearances at the end of next week and a couple of witness interviews scheduled. My newest client, Jean Sheridan, a bookkeeper for a local printing company, stands accused of embezzling more than $200,000 over a five-year period. Seems she's had a bit of a gambling problem. *Maybe I should've given this one to Dolores*, I think to myself. I need to get Beaker to do some fact finding for me, and I begin making a list of things I'd like done by early next week. This one most likely will end in a plea deal. We'll see. I'm almost finished with my list when I hear someone come in.

"Hey," Beaker says sticking his head in my office.

"Hey."

"You okay?"

"Yep, I'm fine. Sleep does wonders," I say trying to make a case for my bizarre behavior yesterday.

"Okay. That's cool."

His response seems way too easy. I'm suspicious, but I certainly can't say any more without giving him another reason to question me, so I quickly say, "I'm starving, you want to join me for breakfast?"

"Sure, let me dump my backpack. I'll meet you up front."

I walk past the kitchen and say hello to Patrick, Missy's husband, who's scooping ice into glasses from the ice machine.

"Oh, hey Bertie, how are ya?" Patrick says with a bright smile. He's a perfect match for Missy. They're both dynamos! These two have more energy than anyone I know, and they'd have to because not only do they run this amazing diner, but they are the parents of eighteen-month-old twins, Charlotte and Maxwell.

"I'm great, can I grab a table?"

"You bet. Sit anywhere you'd like. Someone'll be with you in a minute."

"Thanks, Patrick."

I find a booth and slide in. It's not long before Beaker joins me. Missy sees us and immediately comes over to greet us and places two cups on the table, filling them without the need to ask. We spend the next few minutes catching up. I ask her about the twins. As any proud mother would, she pulls out her phone and shares the latest baby photos. Their twins are darling, blond-haired,

blue-eyed cherubs who are at the age where they probably will leave anyone tending to them breathless and
exhausted in a matter of minutes. I make the obligatory
ooh's and ah's, though I am being sincere. What's not to
love when presented with two angels hugging their new
Golden Retriever puppy? That's, like, double-adorable
and too sweet for words, and I'm happy for Missy and
Patrick, who work hard to build a strong foundation for
their family. It should be this way for everybody. I think
about Annie and wonder what the future will hold for
her, Jack, and the baby. I glance over at Beaker and wonder how he's going to react to the news.

I order a couple eggs over light and wheat toast.
Beaker orders the French toast, which I envy. Our food
arrives and I smile as I see that Missy's snuck in a couple pieces of crispy bacon on my plate. She knows it's
my kryptonite. I think you could add bacon to a leather
shoe and it would be delicious. Beaker and I are halfway
through our meal when Annie slides into the booth next
to me, helping herself to a piece of toast and using my

knife to apply generous amounts of butter and strawberry jam.

"Hungry?" I ask at the intrusion of her fingers in my plate.

"Famished," she says between bites. "Hey, Beaker." She greets him with a mouthful of toast.

"Hey, Annie. You look like you're in a good mood this morning."

"I am." She looks at me with a grin. "So, did you tell him?"

I can see from her face that she's as giddy as a schoolgirl over the pregnancy. But what Beaker's about to find out, will not, I suspect, evoke the reaction she's hoping for. So, I stall, bracing for the inevitable. "What news?" I ask, displaying my best poker face.

"You know very well what news." She's nudging me with her shoulder.

"Ohhhh.... that news," I say, playing it off as if I'm clueless. "Well, that's your news to tell, not mine."

Beaker, who's been sitting there and hasn't put his fork down, finally stops eating and says, "What? What's going on? Do I still have a job?"

"I don't know, Mom. Does he?" Annie says.

"Yes, Beaker, you still have a job. She's pulling your leg."

"Annie, put him out of his misery and tell him," I say.

"How would Uncle Beaker sound to you?" Annie says with a grin.

"I don't know how I'm supposed to respond to that?" He's looking bored with whatever game this is.

"Okay, Beaker, let me say it another way. I'M PREG-NANT!!" She squeals with excitement, clapping her hands.

Beaker shows absolutely no reaction. He stabs another piece of French toast with his fork, stuffs it in his mouth, and says with mouth full, "That's great."

Annie is totally unaware of the bomb she's just exploded on him. She's too lost in her own glee to notice his less-than-enthusiastic response.

She barrels on. "Thank you! Jack and I are so excited. Due in September. We've got a ton of things to do to get ready for him or her. We're waiting to find out the sex. We're just not sure yet whether we want to know or not, you know what I mean? I mean, I know other people want to find out. They do those gender reveal parties, but, oh, I don't know, I mean, I get why people want to find out early, so they can start getting the baby's room ready, but, hey, we don't even know where the baby's room's going to be." She finally stops talking. I'm surprised she hasn't fainted from going so long without taking a breath. I've never seen her like this, except when she found out she'd passed the Bar exam.

I make no attempt to stop the babbling of this first-time mother-to-be. I couldn't if I tried. It'd be like trying to leap into a lightning-fast pair of jump ropes in double-dutch. Beaker is looking down at his plate, continuing to shovel in his breakfast. Annie keeps rambling, totally unaware that half of her audience is in pain right now. "So, whaddaya think?"

He finally stops eating, wipes his mouth on a napkin, and says, "That's great, Annie, that's really great. Happy for the both of you. Hey, listen, I gotta get busy." He gets up and reaches into his back pocket for his wallet.

"I got this, Beaker."

"Oh, thanks." He simply turns and walks back to the offices.

"Well, that was strange. I would expect him to show a little more enthusiasm," Annie says crossing her arms in front of her chest and leaning back, clearly disappointed in his lack of a reaction.

"Annie, did it ever occur to you that he might not be exactly thrilled with your news?" I'm still getting a blank stare, and what I'm trying to communicate to her simply isn't registering. "I don't know how else to say this, because that boy—that man," I say pointing to the empty seat that Beaker just occupied, "has feelings for you."

Her expression alters only slightly. "That's silly. Beaker and I are just friends. We've never been anything but friends."

I just sit and stare at her. For someone so bright, fifth in her class at Vandy, she has been completely clueless when it comes to Beaker, and it also irritates me that she so quickly dismisses what I've told her.

"You sure about that?" I ask.

It takes her a few seconds to let that sink in, and when it does, those beautiful eyes of hers are now two sizes wider than when we began this conversation. "Oh, God, I didn't know. He never gave me any indication that he was interested in anything other than a platonic relationship."

"Annie, it's Beaker." She looks at me confused. I repeat myself again, "It's *Beaker*. He's not like all the other guys. In fact, I would imagine he would likely wait for someone to approach him first. I think he's loved you from a distance forever."

"Oh my God, I feel so stupid for not knowing. How did I not know after all this time? And why didn't you ever say anything?" As if I'm somehow at fault for her cluelessness.

"What? Oh no, I'm not taking responsibility for this one."

"I should go in and talk to him."

"Well, that might be a good idea. He's been a good friend to you, and you to him. Just give him some time. It may take him a while to come to terms with all of it. Now, I've got to get back to work." I throw some cash on the table and scoot in her direction, her cue to get up and out of my way. "Hey, you feelin', okay? Well, besides this?" I gesture again to Beaker's empty seat.

"Yeah, for the most part. I've had some bouts of nausea throughout the day, but nothing too awful."

"I remember those early days I was pregnant with you for sure. I hope you don't experience it for too long. Keep soda crackers in your desk—that's what I did with you." I'm giving her the best advice I have.

"How about you, Mom? How are you doing? Anything I can do for you?"

I choke up a bit at her concern. "No honey, this is just something I've got to deal with. I'm working through stuff, and I promise to sit down with you as soon I can and explain everything. Promise. C'mon, we've got a business to run."

I go back to my office and shut the door. I can hear Beaker and Annie's muffled voices in the other room, and I truly hope Beaker's going to be alright. He's become part of our family, not just our "working family," and I hate to see him hurt. Perhaps in time he'll be fine.

I check my messages and emails and don't find what I'm anticipating. Dammit, this is driving me absolutely nuts. If I don't hear something by the end of the day, I'm going to be making a phone call, which is the last thing I want to do. I turn to the computer and do my best to focus on other things, desperation is my friend right now, forcing me to concentrate. I begin by reviewing documents sent over by the attorneys representing the plaintiffs of the printing company. Voices are still seeping through the door. I ask Google Home to play soft jazz, sultry sounds of a saxophone and the gentle strumming of guitar strings override the voices coming through the door. I close my eyes for a minute, hurting for Beaker. I allow the music to transport me to a place that was a lifetime ago, and I let my mind drift back, to a boy whose heart I abandoned.

1975

EIGHT

Estill County, Kentucky

Audrey's in the back room lying on the cot Mr. Mason keeps for those times when a nap is a necessity. I'm still reeling from her secret. Her father should be horse-whipped. And what about her brothers, do they know what their father's done? Of course they know. If there's one thing I've learned living with Mama, secrets are never really secrets, and the co-conspirators hide the truth, cuz everybody knows, but everybody *ain't* talking. Audrey's situation upsets me more than Eddy's cretin behavior this afternoon. However, I'm not so stupid to let my guard down with that imbecilic gorilla. Jimmy's in back, prepping for the dinner hour. The old guys are still sitting in their booth jawing away. It's been hours now, but I know this is the height of their social activity on a Friday. I look at the clock, only about an hour left until we can get outta here and Helen and the new waitress Sheila take over for the dinner shift. I wipe the counter with the soggy rag for the tenth time and scan the perimeter for anything else to be done. I've filled straw dispensers, napkin holders, salt and pepper shakers, and condiment bottles. Not much else to do. I spy a *Teen Beat* magazine I left under the counter last week, pick it up, and drool over the face of David Cassidy, the heartthrob of every red-blooded American girl, and begin humming "I Think I Love You" to myself. I flip through the magazine trying to curb the boredom that is now threatening to turn me to stone. The bell rings, a new customer. I look up and can't stop smiling.

Every time I see Billy Stivers, he practically takes my breath away. I could never have imagined that my heart would one day belong to that little farm boy who was made to pick his tray up off the cafeteria floor after being subjected to the town bully. Who would have guessed he'd grow up to be the most handsome boy in Estill County? Eddy doesn't mess with Billy anymore, considering that somewhere during the middle school years, this scrawny kid morphed into a tall, lean, extremely healthy young man. The most beautiful thing about Billy is that he doesn't even know how gorgeous he is. That makes him so very sexy.

My heart aches even more now because in a week, I'll be gone. I plan on telling him soon, but I think he suspects I won't be around forever. I love him, I really do, but I don't want to spend the rest of my life here—and he does. He's attending Eastern Kentucky University this fall to pursue his degree in Agricultural Studies. I laugh and tell him that's like sending Santa Claus to the University of Toy Making. He practically runs their forty-acre farm; his father's been a good teacher. It's backbreaking work. He has lofty plans, big dreams. He loves it and aspires to modernize his family's farm with new technology. I know he'll do just that—make it something special. I want him to be happy, but being a farmer's wife, well, that just isn't in the cards for me. He already knows I'm sure, he's just waiting for me to let him down gently.

"Well, what brings you into the big city?" I laugh.

He strolls up to the counter and leans in for a kiss, and I happily consent.

"Pop asked me to come in for some supplies. I thought I'd see if maybe you wanted to do something tonight. I got a whole tank of gas and a little money in my pocket. We could maybe ride over to Lexington. I'll buy you a steak dinner. How about it?"

"That sounds great, really it does, but I promised Audrey and the girls I'd do something with them tonight. How about tomorrow night? You could pick me up here, say around six p.m.?"

"Yeah, we can do that," he says, showing some disappointment. "I was just hoping to see you tonight. We haven't had much time together lately, Bertie. Between the farm and your waitressing, well, you know."

"I know. But I promise, tomorrow, just you and me." I cross my heart with my finger.

"Okay, we can go into Richmond and see a movie if you want to. I hear there's that new one about a killer shark, *Jaws*."

"Aww, you really know how to sweep a girl off her feet! A killer shark, huh," I laugh. "I'd love to!"

Billy and I started dating after winter break this past year. We spent the first half of the school year staring at each other from across the hall. After Christmas, he finally got up the nerve to ask me out. He was shy and beautiful. His incredible smile coupled with the physical transformation from boy to man that took place in high school made him every girl's dream. Another incredible thing about Billy, besides his outward appearance and gentle spirit, is that Mama doesn't even scare him.

It was only the beginning of this summer that he met her. I usually would arrange to meet him outside the house, reducing the chances of entrapment. On this particular evening, I was taking my time to get ready. I wanted to look special for Billy. I was wearing my new black-and-red minidress with black piping and gold buttons down the front. I completed my outfit with a pair of chunky platform sandals the color of the beach. I'd even painted my toenails red. I felt so pretty and was just taking the last of the rollers out of my hair when I heard Mama say, "Well, hello there, gorgeous. *Mmm, mmm, mmm!* Aren't you a looker? You must be Billy? I wasn't even sure if you *was* a real boy. Come on in."

I thought I'd die of embarrassment. Mama using that sickening seductive voice she uses on men to get whatever she wants. I flew down the steps as fast as I could to intervene. There was Mama, wearing her thin bathrobe, hair wrapped in a towel, drink in hand. She had only arrived home a half hour earlier from work.

"Hi, Billy. Well, I see you've met Mama. Okay, well, see you later, don't wait up." Which was a ridiculous thing to say since Mama has never in her life waited up for me. It's the other way 'round.

"Billy, you wanna little drink?" she said, swirling the ice in her glass, the ice clinking against the sides.

"No, thanks, Mrs. Campbell. I'm good."

Mama put on her finest pout and said, "Oh, don't call me Mrs. Campbell, that makes me feel so old. It's Glennis, you can call me Glennis."

"Okay, Glennis," Billy said respectfully.

I grabbed his arm about to steer him out the door when Mama tripped over the rug, spilling her drink down the front of my dress. I couldn't speak, I was so mortified, not to mention ready to tear her limb from limb.

"Oops," she said, laughing as she looked into my eyes. It was no accident. "Let me get you a towel." She weaved her way down the hall to the kitchen.

"Do you want to change? I'll wait," Billy offered.

"Naw, I'll dry, if you don't mind my new perfume." I wanted to get out of there.

"Are you kiddin'? You're talking to someone who spends a whole lotta time in the company of hogs."

"Well then, maybe *you* oughta go up and change. You might have some difficulty finding anything in my closet that works for you, though." I was trying to hide my shame.

In her gin-buzzed voice, Glennis Campbell wished us a good night. She'd already forgotten what she went into the kitchen for.

We were heading to Richmond that night to watch *The Trial of Billy Jack*. On the way, I apologized for Mama's behavior.

"Bertie, you don't have anything to apologize for. You're not responsible for what your mama says or does."

"It's a habit. I've spent my whole life apologizing for her. I'll bet your folks don't think too much of us dating, do they? I mean, you dating the daughter of the town drunk and all."

What he did next startled me. Without warning, he took the next exit, almost on two wheels, finally stopping in a gravel lot. It had belonged to an abandoned building, Leroy's Electrical Repair Shop, where according to the aged and weather-beaten sign, We Can Fix Near Anything.

He threw the truck into park and looked at me with a smoldering intensity I'd never seen in his eyes before. "Now, you listen to me, Bertie Campbell. You got nothin' to be ashamed of. You're the most beautiful, smart, and funny girl I've ever known. My folks raised me to judge people based on their character, and you got miles and miles of that. Don't you let anybody tell you any different."

Tears stung my eyes. I'd never heard anybody champion for me like that before. I knew in that moment that my feelings for him couldn't be denied. "You keep talking like that and I might have to ask you to marry me," I said kiddingly.

He broke out in a big grin and said, "Bertie Campbell, I'd be honored." His expression suddenly changed. "Hey, I just thought of something I'd like to show you before we head into Richmond. Would you mind if we make another stop?"

"Not at all, what is it?"

"Just wait," was all he said.

Billy headed down the highway a couple of miles and got off at the next exit. We traveled another mile or so before he turned off on a narrow gravel back road, the tires crunching. With my anticipation growing, he finally pulled into an area just off the road that looked to be private property. An old and rusty metal gate was positioned across a gravel drive that seemed to just disappear into a cluster of trees. The gate seemed silly because there was nothing stopping a person from walking around it.

"Where are we going? Are we trespassing on someone's property?" I asked, now a little concerned.

"Nah, it's fine I promise. You'll see. Just wait," he repeated.

Billy took my hand, and I walked with him into the warm June evening. The sun hadn't quite set, and its dim glare caused me to shield my eyes with an informal salute of my free hand. We left the gravel path and stepped into a clearing of overgrown vegetation filled with quarter-sized dandelions, ragweed, and furry yellowish-green foxtails that sprung up here and there, towering over the other weeds. I'm sure our unwanted footsteps were disrupting the tiny insect dwellers already settled in for the evening. I felt young and alive, along with another feeling I'd never felt before. I felt sensual. Oh, my God, how my body tingled as if my senses were supercharged. There was something different happening between us tonight, something electric. I knew he was feeling the same way. Nature's volume must have been on high because I was acutely sensitive to all its sounds and movements, especially Billy's. My body could feel the heat radiating from this boy walking next to me.

"Do you really know where you're going?" I asked.

"You'll see," he said with a mischievous smile.

I continued to let him guide me into the thick tree line just ahead. He pulled me into a pocket of open space between the trees. It was instantly cooler in the shade of the dense woods. Beams of light found their way between the tree gaps and I felt like I entered an elaborate movie set, waiting for magical woodland creatures to appear.

"Should I be worried?" I laughed.

"Not when you're with me." He stopped and pulled me to his chest. His kiss was so extraordinary that I was melting into him. I didn't want it to end and I honestly could have stayed there with him, just like this. When he finally released me, I was dizzy and left with a wanting ache.

"C'mon, I've got something to show you." He grabbed me by the forearm, and we began running through the trees. My body was still in shock from the kiss, but I manage to keep my feet moving. We reached the edge of the tree line and burst into the golden evening light. When I could stop and catch my breath, I was astonished at what I saw.

"Where did you ever find this place? I've lived here all my life and I never knew this existed." A wide foaming creek, its waters cascading over huge rocks, was picture perfect. The crown jewel was a tiny waterfall created by layers of centuries-old rock. It looked like something out of a travel magazine. An old tree had fallen over the narrowest part of the creek, forming an organic bridge that gave one access to the other side.

"What do ya think? My folks own this land, and someday," he scanned the land with such pride in his eyes, "well, someday, it'll be mine."

"Oh my God, Billy, it's so beautiful. This should be painted. I've got to tell Eve."

Billy laughed. "That's what I get for showing you this place? 'I've got to tell Eve.'"

"Oh no, I'm sorry, I mean, it's just so beautiful, and well, she's so talented, and..." I stopped. "You're right. I kind of spoiled the moment."

His grin told me he wasn't mad. "Well we can fix that," he said reaching out and grabbing me. That kiss that I had experienced only moments ago returned, but this time, there was no stopping.

"You're so beautiful, Bertie." He was kissing my face, my lips, my throat.

"Oh my God, Billy," I moaned as I gripped my hands in his hair and couldn't control my own actions as I guided his lips to my breasts.

"Are you sure you're okay with this?" he whispered.

"I've never been more sure of anything in my life."

He never took his eyes off me as we slowly made our way to a more secluded spot, closer to the creek.

He stopped and pulled his t-shirt over his head, his shoulders broad and strong. His body was perfection, virile and powerful, like a statue of a Greek god. I was amazed that he had chosen me. Billy took me once again in his arms. He was so gentle, yet very much in command. He slowly unzipped my gin-scented dress, letting it fall to the ground. I stood before him in the last rays of the sun and all I could hear was the rhythm of the creek as the water bubbled over the rocks.

He stepped back and gazed at my body. "Bertie, you're the most beautiful thing I've ever seen."

I was literally on fire as we tumbled to the ground. I didn't care that we were laying on a bed of grass and weeds, dry and brittle from the heat. I didn't care about anything but what was happening at that very moment. Suddenly, everything exploded in my body and I was racked with both pain and pleasure. Seconds later, Billy's body reacted with the same intensity. It hurt so good that a few tears made their way down my cheek. He gently rolled on his side, reached out, and wiped my tears away with his thumb.

"Did I hurt you? Bertie, I'm sorry if I hurt you. Was it okay? Bertie?" The concern in his voice was so tender.

I answered by pulling him close and kissing him. We laid together perfectly still, spooning, naked and unashamed. Billy plucked a foxtail, and, starting at my calf, let it glide up my inner thigh, following the curve of my hip, around my belly, up to my breasts, until it reached my throat. I giggled as it tickled my flesh.

"Oh, does that tickle?" And without waiting for my response, he nuzzled my throat and nibbled my ear. I'd never felt more satisfied or content. I can't remember a time I was ever that happy, when I ever felt truly wanted. "Whatcha thinkin' about?" he asked, running strands of my hair through his fingers.

"How I never want this night to end," I said with a sigh.

"Me neither." A few moments lapsed. "I love you, Bertie."

I remained quiet. My heart began to beat faster. I didn't know how to respond, because his words scared me. Love was foreign to me. I'm supposed to love Mama, but I don't. I love the girls, I love Mr. and Mrs. Mason and the folks at the Good Eats for the support they've given me. But this was not the same. This was an altogether different kind of love. One that requires commitment. I was afraid if I didn't respond, all of this might suddenly be over, and I wasn't ready for that. So, I finally said the words I knew he wanted to hear and that I wanted to believe I meant. "I love you too, Billy."

He held me tighter. "I want to spend the rest of my life with you. You're like no other girl I've ever met. Do you think that's possible, us together, forever?"

I hesitated, and though I was touched by his words, I wanted to be honest with him. "Forever's a long time, Billy." I didn't want to hurt this beautiful boy, but my life up to now had been such a mess. Mama had been such a mess. All I'd ever wanted was to just run away. How do I tell him this? I gently pushed on. "We have each other here and now. I don't know what the future will hold. We both have our own dreams. You're going off to school in the fall. I need to keep working to make enough money to do the same." I switched gears, hoping I could steer the conversation a bit. "Did I tell you I got an acceptance letter to Vandy?"

He immediately sat up. "God, no Bertie! That's unbelievable, why didn't you tell me earlier?" I hadn't told anyone because it was pointless.

"Because I'm not going," I said, matter-of-factly.

"What do you mean you're not going?" He looked at me as if I'd lost my mind. "Bertie, it's Vanderbilt!"

I sat up, reached for my dress, and covered myself. "Because it's impossible, that's why. Do you honestly think I can afford to go? Or that Mama would find a way to help me? I applied because I wanted to know that I could make it into that school. Believe me, I have every intention of someday getting to college, and making something of myself, maybe even as a lawyer. But it'll just have to wait. If anything, I'm practical. I'm not a romantic. I'm a realist—Glennis Campbell taught me how to be that." I could hear the hysteria rise in my voice and felt myself losing control. A swell began in my chest, building up resentful steam that needed to be released, like a pressure cooker. I pulled the dress over my head. I knew he was seeing a side of me I hadn't revealed to him before. He couldn't possibly understand how much I want to have a life like everyone else, college, love, a career, and eventually a family. But I have to get out of Estill County to do it. I couldn't tell him that. I really didn't want to hurt him, and I was afraid I might have just thrown cold water on his hopes of us being together, forever. But instead of being upset, he did something pretty amazing. He wrapped his arms around me.

"You'll get there, Bertie Campbell. You'll get everything you want, everything you deserve. I just know you will. I won't pressure you. I won't push. Just know that I love you, and I will for the rest of my life."

"Bertie, Bertie? Hello, I think I've lost ya!" Billy waves his hand in front of my face, attempting to bring me out of my trance.

"Oh sorry, what were you saying?"

"The movies. *Jaws* tomorrow night?"

"Oh yeah, yes, that'll be great. Tomorrow around six. I'll be waiting."

"You better keep that girl safe," Mr. Rader barks from his booth. I almost forgot Mr. Rader and his buddies are still here.

"What's that?" Billy asks, turning to the men.

"Mr. Rader, now, I'm going to have to charge you rent if you're here much longer," I tease.

"You're girlfriend's just got into a tangle with a fella. He's a mean one, that fella," Mr. Rader says.

"What's he talkin' about?" Billy asks in a low voice, turning back to me.

"Oh, it's nothin'. Eddy just came in here looking for Marie and started shootin' off his mouth as always. Jimmy took care of it. Eddy ran outta here with his tail, 'tween his legs," I laughed.

"You be careful, Bertie, you hear me?" he said seriously. "I mean it."

"I will, I promise. Don't you worry any. I know how to handle myself. You know as well as I do that I've had lots of experience dealing with unpleasant folk," I say. "I can take care of myself, and besides, I know where to find ya if I need help. Now, let me get back to work."

"You mean droolin' over that guy in the magazine," he teases. "Okay, I'll leave ya to it." He says as he leans over the counter and kisses me goodbye.

Present Day

NINE

That would be the last time I kissed that boy, a boy who was the spitting image of the only other man I would ever love, Joe.

My train of thought is interrupted by a knock on my office door. "Come in."

"Hey, have you heard from Dolores?" Beaker asked with concern in his voice.

"No, why?"

"Well, it's almost ten, and she's not in yet."

"Really? Oh! I hope she's alright. Let me give her call."

I try her cell several times, but it just keeps going to voicemail. I try her landline. The recorder picks up with Dolores's distinct, deep voice. *"I'm not here. Leave a message. Not a long one."* You'd never hire Dolores as a receptionist. What she lacks in cordial pleasantries, she

147

makes up for in grit and determination. Now *I'm* worried. I find the number for the main office of the Willows and ask them to go check on her. They promise to call me back and let me know what they find out.

I wring my hands for what seems like forever. Beaker and Annie haven't left my office. They're as anxious as I am to hear something. When my cellphone rings, we all jump, and I grab it.

"Oh, God! When you find out where they're taking her, call me back. Okay, thanks." I hang up and see the concern etched in their faces. "They found her unresponsive on the floor of her bathroom. An ambulance is on the way. They'll call me back as soon as they know which hospital she'll be transported to. I just pray they're not too late."

It's been a long afternoon and an even longer evening as I sit in Dolores's darkened hospital room where she's now sleeping peacefully from what they've said was a mild heart attack. From what I've been able to deduce, they're worried because of her age, and since I'm not family, they can't tell me much more. I did overhear them say something about running more tests, but for tonight, they're monitoring her closely. I've called her sister in Detroit, and she and her son have arranged a flight that gets in sometime tomorrow afternoon. I've sent Beaker and Annie home. Luckily, we decided to drive separately before heading over. I want to stay with her tonight; besides, she seems to be resting comfortably. This barracuda looks peaceful right now. *It's amazing what a tranquilizer gun can do.* The doctor said he'd never seen anyone who was so combative after suffering a heart attack, even a mild one. She's a feisty one, I told him, don't take it personally, the heart attack has absolutely nothing to do with her charming disposition. I told him she was crowned Miss Congeniality of her senior class—he didn't take the bait.

It's now about ten p.m., and I'm sitting in a freezing room that reeks of disinfectant and is clearly not doing its job of overriding the smell of urine. There's a good reason I never went into the medical field, and I'm grateful for those who did. My teeth are chattering, and I've wrapped myself in a hospital blanket that feels like a burlap sack, as if it's been continuously washed in bleach without the use of fabric softener. It's noisy in the hallway, I've left the door cracked so that I'm not completely in the dark. I don't want to chance turning on a light and waking her. Bells keep going off, someone's paging Doctor Levinson for the third time. "Damn, Doctor Levinson, answer your page," I say under my breath. There's an in-depth conversation about easy crockpot meals at the nurses' station, and carts are being wheeled up and down the hallway. Dolores is snoring, lucky her. And I'm worried about turning on a light for fear of waking her, *jeez*.

I change positions and try to get a little more comfortable. I'm literally sitting on my phone, so I reach down and free it from under my butt. I set it on my lap and close my eyes. There's a ping from the phone and my lap lights up causing me to have to disentangle my hand from under the blanket to retrieve it. I'm assuming that it's a text from Annie or Beaker checking in. I glance down, but it's just my cellular service thanking me for my auto payment. I go ahead and check for any furthers messages or emails I might have missed in the last couple hours. I begin scrolling my emails when I see it sitting in my inbox since 8:53 p.m. The subject once again is "Fireflies." I brace myself for what is just on the other side of a single tap. A jittery tap, and I read the following message: *Let's meet. Wednesday, April 15 @ 11:00 a.m. 11847 Benton Way, Arlington, VA. Signed, A.* My heart is beating, but I now know who's trying to reach me. "So, it's you, Audrey," I say out loud, almost relieved.

"What are you mumblin' about?"

I'm startled by Dolores's voice. "Oh, hey lady. You gave us a scare. How ya feelin'?" I say, getting up and standing by her bedside. I'm still freezing, so I keep the blanket around me.

"Yunno, thassa really dumb queshun."

"Shh, sorry, you don't have to talk. Why don't you just rest?" I say. She's groggy from the meds or quite possibly... I don't want to think that she's suffered another blow.

"Who's Audrey?" she says, catching me off guard.

It takes me a second to respond. "Wow, nothing's wrong with your hearing. She's just an old friend," I say.

"Aww, yeah, Audrey." She slightly laughs and then coughs.

I don't know what she means by that, but I'm thinking she's still in her drug-induced la-la land. "Let me see if you're able to have some water." I push her call button and ask the nurse.

Moments later the nurse arrives, checks her vitals, and asks if she'd like something to drink. I step out and give her time to tend to Dolores. I take a stroll down the hall and stop at the large plate-glass windows that span the waiting area directly across from the elevators. The chairs are upholstered in a greenish-gray fabric with a light chartreuse color in a swirl pattern. The flooring is of a beige-ish gray linoleum. I make a mental not to seek decorating tips from whomever they hired to do this job. It's raining and water droplets have formed on the large panes. I walk over to the window and stare out, watching the cars travel along the street in front of the hospital, headlights displaying the sheets of rain coming down. I realize I still have the blanket wrapped around me. My thoughts turn to the email I just received. I now know it's Audrey and that she still lives and works in the D.C. area. I've tried keeping up with all of them over the years, from a distance, of course. But Audrey—I think about her the most. I miss her. I miss my best friend. I sigh... I don't want to be gone too long from Dolores, so I head back to the room. The nurse has left, and Dolores is upright.

"Hi." I approach the bed.

"Thought maybe you ran away to avoid my que-shunns." She's more alert now than she was when I left her with the nurse. Her speech is better. Slow, still a bit of a slur, but not as affected as I feared.

"Nope. I was just giving the nurse a chance to do her thing. Can I getcha anything?"

"No. Why don't you tell me wass goin'on?"

"Well, you've had a mild heart attack."

"Oh, hell, I know that. I'm not talkin' bout that. I'm talkin' bout *you*. Wass goin' on with you?"

I realize I'm not getting off the hook. "I've never been able to keep much from you, have I, Dolores?"

She ignores me. "Start with this Audrey person, then tell me wasso important about a green box."

I stand in the dark, contemplating the best approach to her question, knowing she's not going to let me get by saying nothing, or brushing it off as if it's nothing of consequence. Dolores is way too smart for that, so I do my best to answer her truthfully. "Oh, Dolores, I don't even know where to begin. It's all so ridiculously messy and complicated, not to mention so long ago that I have a hard time remembering it all. But more than that, I'm afraid you're going to think less of me." I confess with the sorrow of a swollen heart I haven't felt in years.

"Lemme tell you somethin'," she says, her voice quiet but raspy. "Do ya really think I'd work with someone without knowing a little somethin' about 'em?"

It takes me a minute. "Are you saying...?"

"Yep, I know about you, Bertie Campbell." The shock of hearing Dolores say that name is almost too much to bear.

"Dolores, I...you...." I can't even formulate a sentence; I'm caught unaware.

Dolores chuckles and then coughs. "What? You think you're the only one who has secrets? We all do. But you don't have to worry, Bertie. I'd never betray ya."

"So, you know?" I ask, still dumbfounded.

"I know of some... *things*."

"Hold on. Why on earth did you ever decide to work with me if you knew about my past?"

"Well," she paused. "Two reasons. One, cuz there's never one side to any story, and two, anyone who's managed to rise from the ashes, like I think you have, starting a new life and all, well, that's the kinda person who's got grit and d'termination, and I admire that. You've gotta a fightin' spirit." She stopped to gather her thoughts and find her words. "After my stroke, nobody wanted me anymore. I mean *no*body. I'd worked so hard provin' that a woman could be just as good a lawyer as any man, if not better, and then look what happens, I go and have a stroke. Was it fate? Hell no, it just happened. Life's not fair, Bertie, but you know as well as I do it's all about what ya do under those circumstances that decides your future. You're like me—you take control. I knew I had so much more to give, and I wasn't gonna let that stroke define me. Or stop me. I wasn't finished. Then one day, I stumbled upon you. Like I said, I don't believe in fate or any of that crap." She stops and coughs a bit and I bring her water, adjusting the straw for her to sip, before she bats it away, clears her throat, and continues, still sounding a bit hoarse. "We made our own opportunities, you and me. I dunno your whole story, Bertie, or everything that's happened to ya, but I'll bet you've been carrying somethin' almost malignant inside ya for a very long time, something that's eating at your very core and ya need to set it free. So, maybe it's time for ya to unburden yourself. You might as well pull up a seat and tell me, cause I'm not going anywhere. You can start whenever you're ready."

"Dolores, you're a good friend." I move over to the chair and sit down, wrapping the blanket around me even tighter. "Well, I guess I should begin with the night it all started and tell you about three very special friends."

1975

TEN

Estill County, Kentucky

"We're leaving now. Meet us out front in ten minutes," I say to Eve over the phone. I hang up and turn to Audrey, who's sitting on the cot, tying her shoes. "They're at Eve's. Marie's been hiding out there for most the day while Eve was working at the store. She said Eddy came by the hardware store looking for Marie. I guess he started getting stupid, so Eve's parents asked him to leave. Marie heard his car drive by the house about an hour ago. We better watch out for him just to be safe." I pause for a moment. "I really don't get Marie," I confess, "it seems like an awful lot to go through, just to have one night to yourself, for cryin' out loud. I wish she'd dump that loser." I look at Audrey, who hasn't said a word. In fact, I'm not sure she's even heard anything I've said. "You sure you're feeling up to this?" I ask again.

"Yeah, I'm fine. Let's get outta here," she says, jumping off the cot and handing me my bag.

We've already changed into the outfits we're wearing for tonight's girls' night. Audrey has on a low-cut blue tank top and a pair of short, white denim shorts. She looks good, even for being sick for the better part of the day. Audrey's long legs go on forever and her thick red hair looks like shimmering copper against her navy tank. I'm wearing, once again, my peasant blouse and cut-off jeans. I haven't seen as much as a ray of the sun this summer. With all the shifts I've picked up at the diner, there hasn't been much time left for sunbathing. Between my chalky-white complexion and long black hair, I have a strong resemblance to Lillian Munster.

"Okay, let's do this. We got everything?" I ask, checking the area just to make sure.

Jimmy's busy grabbing orders off the carousel with one hand and flipping burgers on the griddle with the other. Helen's barking out the next round of orders. The diner's filling up with the usual crowd for a Friday night. Many ladies in town get a break from cooking at least one evening a week, thanks to the Good Eats. Audrey and I head out the back door. "Jimmy, we're outta here. I'll see you tomorrow."

I'm scheduled to work in the morning, which is a good reminder that I'd better not get too crazy tonight, or I'll have hell to pay with my head in the morning. I wonder how Mama drinks like she does only to get up, go to work, and do it all over again—day in, day out, night after night. It's not unusual to see her having a drink at the breakfast table before work. What's she call it? My little morning pick-me-up, I think.

"Hold up," Jimmy says, wiping his hands on his apron. He reaches under the counter and hands me a large paper bag. "Here, this oughta keep you from starving tonight."

"Oh gosh, I almost forgot," I say taking the sack from Jimmy. The bag's warm. I open it and peek in. Before I can inspect its contents, the smell of ecstasy hits me full in the face. We've struck the motherload. The aroma of hot roast beef sandwiches causes me to salivate. My physical reaction's like that of Pavlov's dog. I examine inside the bag closer, and there's also pickle spears, chips, and thick slices of apple pie. He's gone and made this special for us. I close the bag and do something that even surprises me. I throw my arms around his neck and laughingly say, "Jimmy, you're our angel." I plant a kiss on his check.

He looks about as startled as I am. I've never been the demonstrative kind. I must get that from Mama. His face softens, and he says with a toothless grin, "Darlin, believe me, I ain't no angel."

I laugh and say, "Well, you are to me!" I grab the bag. "Bye!"

I hear his parting words as we leave. "You ladies stay safe."

"We will," I yell back as the screen door slams.

Audrey's parked her little yellow '67 Comet just around the corner from the diner. She's the only one of the four of us who has a car. Her daddy bought it from a used-car dealer in Lexington sometime around her sixteenth birthday. Her brothers are the age where they need to be shuttled around for baseball and basketball games, among other things. She's responsible for taking them where they need to go. She says she has a feeling that once her brother Tom turns sixteen, which will be next year, her daddy will turn the car over to him, and she'll be without any wheels. It's a damn man's world!

We throw our stuff into the trunk, but I place the food bag in the center of the back seat. "Why don't you let me drive? You can just sit back and rest," I say to her, holding my hand out for the keys.

"No, I told you Bertie, I'm fine," she says shaking her head. "I'm pregnant, not sick—well, not this minute, anyway. Besides, Marie and Eve will think it's weird you're driving my car."

"I guess you're right," I say, walking around to the passenger side.

It feels like an oven in the car, and we can't roll down the windows fast enough. The back of our thighs are on fire from the scorching seats. "Here, sit on this." I pull my uniform out of my bag and hand it to Audrey, hoping it will shield her legs from the burning upholstery. I pull my knees up to avoid the red-hot seat.

Audrey starts the engine, but before pulling out, she says, "Bertie, I know I probably don't need to say this, but please don't say anything to them about me being pregnant."

"I've already told you that I won't say a word to anyone. I promise. Stop worrying, would you?"

"Yeah, that's real easy for you to say," she counters.

"Hey, I'm sorry. I know this isn't easy. But it's going to be okay. I promise you, I'll help you. We're going to figure this out—that I promise. So, just for tonight, put it out of your head. Allow yourself some fun. Tomorrow we'll come up with a plan. But for tonight WE BITCHES RIDE!" I am trying to get her to smile.

Audrey finally breaks out in a grin, then nods. "Let's do this!"

Eve's house is just a few blocks away. We pull up front. "Wait here. Let me make sure Eddy's not lurking around, ready to jump out behind a bush or something," I say with humor, but also a bit of trepidation. I cautiously approach the front porch, scanning the area for a possible Eddy sighting. It looks like the coast is clear. Before I even reach the front door, Eve and Marie are bounding down the front steps, racing for the car, gear in hand.

Marie has blankets draped over her arm, and a small cooler in the other hand. It must be heavier than it looks because she seems to be struggling. When I look down at her feet, I realize she's wearing her platform sandals. Just like Marie to put beauty before comfort.

"You know you're gonna twist an ankle in those things down at the river."

"I'm good," she says, ignoring me. "Here, take these blankets, it's hotter than hell hauling these dang things." She hands me her load.

Eve, as always, is trailing behind. She's carrying a huge canvas bag hanging off her shoulder by only one of the straps. Her tennis shoe is untied, and her tortoise-shell glasses are sliding down her nose. The bag she's carrying is bulging from whatever she's stuffed inside. I look at these two and wonder how in the world they ever stayed best friends this long. Talk about peculiar!

We load the stuff in the trunk and quickly hop into the car.

"Oh my God, what smells so good?" Without waiting for an answer, Marie's nose is now in the bag, pulling out the wrapped sandwiches. She tears open the paper and begins ravaging one of the sandwiches. Eve and I watch in wonder. I've never seen anyone put that much food in their mouth at one time. She stops for a moment, mouth full, and says, "What? I'm starving."

"We can tell," I say laughing.

"Here, y'all gotta try these," she says passing one to Eve, then handing me a couple. "My God! These are great."

"You know, I brought these for later down at the river," I say with a smile.

"Nah, let's eat now, besides they're better fresh," she says, returning to pillage what's left in the bag. "Oh my God, there's PIE!"

Now we've all lost it and can't stop laughing. Marie, there's nobody like her. This impulsive, fearless, free spirit is a treasure that the rest of us must constantly monitor, just to keep her safe. "Hey y'all, it's too early to go to the river just yet, whadaya say we head to Richmond for a bit, maybe go to one of the bars, hang out for a while and wait til it gets darker? C'mon, whadaya say, Eve? How 'bout it?"

"I've never been to a bar. What if they don't let us in?" Eve says.

"Oh my God, Eve, have you been livin' under a rock? Have I not taught you nothin'? How many times have I told you about me going up to Richmond, playin' with them college boys from Eastern? Where'd you think I've done my cavortin'?"

"Guess I never thought about it," Eve answered meekly with a shrug of her shoulders.

"Well, duh! Think about it. You can get into the bars if you're eighteen, which we are. You just show 'em your I.D. and get your hand stamped. If you're twenty-one, they don't stamp your hand. Which is pretty fucking stupid if you ask me 'cause it sure don't stop anybody from drinkin'. Any one of them college boys is more than happy to buy you a drink." She throws her head back and laughs. "Sometimes I feel guilty 'cause it's just so easy."

Eve looks kinda scared. "What about it? Eve, Audrey, you up for a little adventure?" I ask. "We do have the rest of the night. It kinda sounds like fun."

"I guess," Audrey says, showing little enthusiasm.

I realize Audrey may not be up for it. "I mean, we don't have to."

"Yeah, we do! It's time this little lady right here gets her first bar experience," Marie says, slapping Eve's thigh. "C'mon, it'll be fun!"

I look at Eve, then Audrey. They both nod yes. "Okay, Richmond it is," I say.

Richmond's less than thirty minutes away on 52W. It's the closest big city from Estill County, and home to Eastern Kentucky University. It's where kids from our little towns travel to when they want to go to the mall or catch a new movie at the theater. It's the one place outside of Estill County that most parents allow their kids to travel on their own. Lexington's a bit further, and the University of Kentucky's a bit larger. We still make it to Lexington occasionally, just most the time with parental permission. Well, I say *we*, but Mama could care less where I go, and my friends envy me because of it. They just don't know that down deep inside it would be nice to have someone in my life who cared where I was. For the rest of the trip, Marie entertains us with her latest antics.

My side is aching from laughing so hard. "Marie, really, stop! I can't take it anymore." I am catching my breath between giggles.

"I'm serious as a heart attack, I've never seen a dick as crooked as that. I mean, it looked like it could use a crutch. I swear. I told him to put it back in his pants and save it for somebody at the VA hospital to look at, cause he could probably get disability for that thing."

I'm laughing so hard now that I can feel my bladder lose control. "Stop, oh my God, stop!" We're wiping our eyes from the tears. I don't think I've ever seen Eve laugh that hard either. I suddenly realize why Marie's Eve's best friend. In some strange way, they fill a void in each other. It makes sense now.

Audrey parks the car down the street from the Bull's Eye, one of the most popular bars off campus. Kids, most likely from the university, are standing in line in front of the bar, waiting to get in. Some are just hanging around the front smoking cigarettes, talking, and generally checking each other out.

Marie leads the way. Red tube top on display, *check*, ample sway in her walk, *check*, short shorts exposing the briefest hint of her ass, *check*. I'm confident we're not going to have a bit of a trouble getting whatever we want tonight. Eve's right behind Marie, looking like a scared ferret, using her right index finger to push up her glasses that are sliding down her nose. Audrey's behind Eve in line.

She shows no emotion. She might as well be standing in line at a drugstore getting a prescription filled. I can't even imagine what's going through her head. Well, I guess I *can* imagine, it's just too awful to think about. I was serious when I said I'll be there for her. This time next week, we'll both be heading for Nashville. The line's at least moving, and I don't mind being the caboose on this train.

"Hey," comes a voice from behind me.

I turn around to see a nice-looking guy with a great head of wavy brown hair and kind eyes. "Hi," I say.

"You been waiting long?" he asks.

"No, my friends and I, we just got here."

"Cool, cool," he says. There's an awkward moment. "Um, so, do you come here much?

I almost laugh at his lame attempt at conversation. "No, nope, this is my first time."

"Oh, really? What are you, like, going to be a freshman this semester?

"Yep, guilty," I lie.

"So, have you decided on a major yet?" he asks.

"Uh," I stall, trying to figure out how to respond. "Political science?" I say more as a question. I turn to Audrey and give her that look of *Oh shit, I hope he doesn't ask any more questions.*

"Oh cool, like maybe running for office, a mayor or something?" He doesn't even wait for my response. "I'm in the law enforcement program. This'll be my second year."

"Oh, wow, that's really cool," I say as I take small steps to back away from him. I turn around to see Marie, Eve, and Audrey looking at me. I turn back to him. I don't want to appear rude, and if I look at their faces, I'll lose it. "So, you're going to be a police officer?"

"Yeah, my dad's a cop, my uncle's a cop, my older brother's a cop, so...you get the picture," he smiles.

"Uh, let me see, so, you're going to be a cop!" I fake a laugh.

He smiles at my feeble attempt at humor. "Yeah, something like that. What dorm are you going to be in this fall?" he asks.

"What dorm? Oh I—" and without completing the sentence, the bouncer asks for my ID. *Thank God!* I show him my driver's license and leave police boy standing at the door.

We spend the next hour and a half really having fun. Marie's managed to score us several rounds of drinks, even though Audrey is sticking to Coke. Eve's even loosened up. As anticipated, Marie's holding court before several of the university boys. It's like watching sweat bees gather around an open soda can at a summer picnic. How quickly that girl can attract them! She's absolutely right, it's so unbelievably easy for her. I look over at Audrey, who's leaning against the wall, not looking so good. It's time to get her out of here. I go over and tell her, "I'm going to round up Marie and Eve. Wait here, I'll be right back." She simply nods.

Marie's sitting at a table with three guys. I wave to her, trying to get her attention. I swear, I think she sees me but she's ignoring me. I look over in the corner, and there's Eve, talking to a fella. He's about her height, his long dark hair covering one eye. It's loud in the bar, so his lips are up close to her ear. She looks happy. I hate to break up the party, but Audrey's had enough. I signal to both Eve and Marie that we're leaving. Eve immediately reacts and looks disappointed, so does the guy she's been cozy with. Bummer. Marie, on the other hand, holds up a finger to indicate *just a minute*. I wave goodbye so she knows we're leaving, and I'm serious. That does the trick. She takes a last gulp of her drink and gets up. The guy sitting next to her reaches out and grabs her by the arm. Marie immediately removes his arm, gives him her best sexy smile, and blows him a kiss.

We're almost to the door when someone from behind yells, "Hey, Eve! wait up!" It's the boy she's been talking to the entire night. Eve turns around. "Can I have your number?" he asks with genuine anticipation in his eyes.

Marie, Audrey, and I look at Eve, and without hesitation, and in unison we say, "Yes, you can!"

Present Day

ELEVEN

I'm stiff and shift in my chair. My throat is dry, my neck is sore, and I need a break. I'm about to tell her I've got to get up for a minute to stretch and find a bathroom when I hear Dolores snoring. I'm relieved. Not only that I can stop my story before she hears what's coming, but because she's been through so much today and needs her rest. Who knows? She may well have forgotten this conversation by tomorrow. I'm kidding myself. Dolores doesn't forget anything.

I get up, stretch, and make my way down the corridor past the nurses' station. I find a bathroom, then just stroll the halls for a bit. Hospitals are strange places at night. It's like this whole other world, completely isolated from the rest of humanity. Even the lighting in the halls casts a strange ghoulish glow, and there's these miniscule flickers of light that keep bouncing around, playing tricks with my vision. I walk back and ask one of the nurses behind the desk where I might get some coffee. She points to a door around the corner and tells me to help myself. I'm grateful. I find the coffee pot and pour myself a generous cup. I'm not going to sleep anyway, so I figure I might as well try and get some things done. I've got to send out emails letting folks know I'll be out of town for a few days next week. How do I explain my sudden travel plans to Annie? I'll figure it out. I'll be as honest as I can with her, but I know she's going to ask a million questions that I simply don't have any answers for. I'll have to get a flight and make hotel reservations. Do I rent a car? I don't even know how long I'll be gone. Is this going to be a quick in-and-out? I don't know what to expect and it terrifies me. And yet, I've got to deal with what's coming. I'll need to make some arrangements for Simone while I'm gone. Beaker was good enough to run by the house tonight and feed her. Wonder if he'd take care of her for a few days. If not, I can have my vet board her, but Simone's not going to be happy if that's the alternative. Oh well, we all gotta do things we don't want to do.

I enter Dolores's room as quietly as possible. She's deeply asleep. I get back in the chair, draping the blanket over my shoulders. I sip my coffee and Google flights to Arlington. After a half hour or so, my vision begins to blur. I set my cellphone down, lean my head back against the chair, and close my eyes. The room's dark with the door closed and the nighttime hospital sounds are now set to a low volume. All I really hear is the beeping of the heart monitor and Dolores herself, and those are both good sounds.

I wake to a jovial voice saying, "Good morning, Ms. Bell, my name's Frances, and I'll be your nurse today."

I open one eye, trying to ease into the morning fog and focus hard on remembering where I am and why my neck's so stiff. Rubbing my eyes, I clear my vision enough to really see nurse Frances, and though she looks to be in her fifties, she has a face that is startling. She could easily be featured on the cover of *Vogue* with her gorgeous mane of jet-black hair pulled back, revealing a flawless ebony complexion. She has incredibly large almond-shaped eyes the color of dark toffee and full sensual lips. Mental note to self: avoid all mirrors this morning if possible.

"How you doin' this morning?" Frances chirps pleasantly. Dolores rewards her with a low growl.

"She's had her rabies shot," I say yawning.

"Aw, well, now, Ms. Bell, is that any way to treat the very folks who are here to help you?"

"If you want to help me, you'll stop fussing over me. I don't like to be fussed over," she bristles.

"She's right—she doesn't," I say, giving Frances a wink.

"Then you're sure as shooting in the wrong place," Frances replies with a wide smile, not intimidated the least by Dolores's gruff exterior. I'll bet Frances most likely deals with her share of crusty old birds on an hourly basis. Dolores doesn't scare her.

"Okay, Ms. Bell, your breakfast should be arriving soon. I'll check in on you a little later."

Dolores doesn't respond. I know how difficult this must be for her. Even at eighty-two, Dolores lets nothing slow her down. This, well, this is going to slow her down a bit. Maybe not for long, but for a bit. Last night, when I wasn't obsessing over my other issue, I was thinking about Dolores's health and how it will affect the firm. I've come to the realization that it's time to add another lawyer to the team. With Dolores's health problems and Annie now pregnant, we're going to need an extra pair of hands. Looks like I'm going to have to have a serious sit-down with Annie and Beaker very soon.

I'm lost in my thoughts when Dolores's cardiologist comes in. I briefly exchange a few words with him, letting him know that her sister and nephew will be arriving sometime today. I excuse myself to give them privacy, and before I'm barely out the door I hear Dolores say, "So, when can I get the hell outta here?"

I take the elevator to the second floor and follow the signs to the cafeteria. I enter an ocean of light-blue scrubs, along with scores of monogrammed white coats, most likely discussing the latest life-saving treatments or the best resort in the Bahamas. I watch as hospital personnel and visitors like myself move about in a morning fog. They meander around the various food stations with trays in hand, necks outstretched, scanning the muffins, bagels, and scrambled eggs, trying to decide what to have for breakfast in this food court extravaganza. Sometimes, when I go into places like this, I feel overwhelmed and get lost in the abundance. For this very reason, I keep it simple this morning. I pay for my simple meal and laugh at myself for using a tray when all I have is a banana and a medium coffee. Oh, well. I find a seat close to the exit and call Annie.

"Hi, it's me."

"I was just getting ready to call you. How's Dolores?" Annie asks.

"Cantankerous, ornery...ya know, Dolores." I start peeling my breakfast and take a bite. "Other than that, she seems to be holding her own, but they're not telling me much, which I understand. Listen, I'm going to stay until the family arrives, which will most likely be around noon. When her sister arrives, maybe she'll be able to get some more information from the cardiologist. I'm going to go home and take a shower and head into the office after that. Can you and Beaker hold down the fort?"

"Absolutely. We got it covered. I think he's heading to the hospital as we speak. But we'll take care of things today."

"Thanks, honey, how are you feeling?" I ask.

"Other than spending this morning with my head in the toilet, just terrific. They say morning sickness is usually a sign of a healthy pregnancy, so I'm trying to keep that in mind every time I heave."

I laugh. "That's a good attitude. I know it's tough, but it usually doesn't last too awfully long."

"Let's hope not. Changing the subject, Jack and I were wondering if you'd like to join us for dinner Saturday night. Maybe try and get reservations at the new restaurant that just opened in Nulu?" In the last couple years, Nulu's exploded with hot new restaurants, bars, galleries, and retail shops, making it an attractive and exciting part of town—the East Market district of Louisville. "I think it's time that you get to know Jack a little better. You know, get acquainted with him outside of court, meet the person who's not your nemesis. What do you think?"

I'm silent for a moment.

"Mom, you there?"

"I'm here."

"Well? What do you think? You up for it?" Annie doesn't push. I love that about her. She's asking, not pushing.

"Sure, hon, absolutely. Just let me know the time and place, and I'll be there."

"That's great, Mom, I really appreciate you making the effort. I promise you're going to love him. Well, maybe. I can't promise that, but I'm hoping."

"Stop worrying, Annie. It's all good. I look forward to it. Of course, you do realize that the gloves will remain on if I have to go up against him in court in the future?" I'm trying to keep it light, but I've gotta be honest.

"Got it. But Saturday, leave the gloves at home."

"Got it. Unless, of course, the temperature drops," I say. "Talk with you later. Love you."

"Love you, too! I'll see you sometime this afternoon."

She has no idea that part of the problem I have with Jack really isn't his personality, it's his profession. That's all I need is a son-in-law who's a prosecutor. I know I'm getting way ahead of myself. Jack was kidding, at least I think he was, when he made the crack in the courtroom before the Davies verdict about being my future son-in-law, but with this baby coming, well, it's possible. I need to defer my worries for another time. I've already got too much on my plate.

When I get back to the room, sure enough Beaker's there. He's brought Dolores the latest racing form. She's sitting up studying it intensely, pencil in hand.

"Well, hi there, you two. What are you up to?" I ask.

"The usual," is all Dolores says. She makes several marks on the form and hands it back to Beaker. "Here, these."

I see she hasn't touched a thing on her breakfast tray. "Are you going to eat? You need to keep up your strength."

"There's nothing on that tray that I want. Beaker, go get me an Egg McMuffin, would ya?"

"Don't you dare, Beaker."

Beaker throws his hands up and says, "I'm not getting in the middle of this." Then he turns to his partner in crime and mouths something I can't quite make out, but I get the gist. Dolores gives him the thumbs up.

"Okay, you win. It's your heart," I say.

"You're damn right," she retorts.

These two have a relationship that's hard to explain. There's nothing maternal on Dolores's part, not one maternal bone in her body. She doesn't see Beaker as a kind of a son. No, not at all. And Beaker's not the least bit interested in lending a hand to an elderly person, whether it's possibly giving assistance as they cross the street, or helping them with, let's say, their groceries. Beaker's just not your guy. I've heard him on the phone with his own mother, and all indications are that he loves her and will help her when asked. Other than that, he appears to have no interest in playing good Samaritan, unless you specifically ask him to do so or give him a little prompting—well, sometimes a big shove. But these two share a kindred spirit and speak a language that the rest of us just don't get. I know beyond a shadow of a doubt that Beaker would do anything for Dolores, and vice versa.

"Well, I gotta go. See you in the office. I'm assuming you're coming in?" Beaker asks.

"Yes, this afternoon. Here, let me walk you out."

"I know what you're doing, Bertie, you're getting him out of here so you can talk behind my back!" she barks.

"So, what if I am? What are you gonna do about it?"

"Hmph."

Beaker and I walk to the elevators, and I ask him to see about blocking some time out later this afternoon, maybe about an hour, for me to speak with him and Annie. I assure him it's nothing dire, but that we need to touch base on a few things.

"If you can, reschedule my afternoon appointment at 3:30, okay? Explain to them that an emergency has come up. I'm hoping to be in the office before then, but it really depends on how soon Dolores's sister gets here. I don't want to leave her alone, and I'm definitely in need of a shower before coming in." Beaker doesn't say a word, just looks at me and nods. "I guess that's it. Any questions?"

"Nope," he says and pushes the button for the elevator. The door opens and he gets in and without saying anything else, he disappears behind closed doors.

"Guess we're done," I say to the closed elevator doors.

I get back to the room, and Dolores is watching the news. She picks up the remote and turns it off. "I've seen enough." I know better than to ask her how she's feeling. I wouldn't get a straight answer anyway.

She's staring at me. "What?" I ask.

"When you gonna finish your story?" she asks.

"Thought maybe you'd forget about that." I'm making a poor attempt at humor.

"Fat chance. Sit down and begin where you left off. I believe you girls were leaving the bar."

"Gee, I thought you'd fallen asleep long before I got to that part." Once again, she just stares at me. "Dolores, you know this is really hard for me."

"I know. That's why you've got to talk to someone. I'm as good a person as any."

And so I begin again, only this time, it's the hardest part.

1975

TWELVE

Estill County, Kentucky

"Sweet Jesus! Who'd a thought this little girl right here would score before all of us?" Marie shouts with enthusiasm, hugging Eve in the back seat. "Now, you gotta admit you had a nice time. C'mon, confess! You did, didn't you?"

Eve finally lets out a giggle. "Yeah, I guess I did?"

"See? I knew it, I just knew you'd have a good time tonight," Marie says, giddy with the thought of a new flirtation.

"So, what's his name, Eve?" I pry.

With just a moment of hesitation she says, "It's Bruce."

We all bust out laughing, unable to contain ourselves. If Eve isn't already embarrassed, she's definitely feeling it now, with our uncontrollable fits of laughter. We're not drunk—well, Marie probably is, but we're feeling no pain and are really, really happy for Eve. But we're not doing a very good job of showing it.

"Bruce? Your knight in shining armor, your Prince Charming's name is Bruce?" I can't stop laughing and the tears are streaming down my face. I look over at Audrey whose reaction is the same.

"Y'all stop makin' fun of me. I mean it now, stop laughing!" Even she can't stop herself from smiling; she's protesting with about as much force as a baby chick. Eve just doesn't have it in her to be mad at us.

"Oh, Eve, we're just kidding with you! You know we love ya," I said, wiping the tears away.

"I know," she admits.

"We really do think it's great. I hope he calls you." It's time for me to let it go. Eve's like our little sister, even though we're the same age. We'd never want to hurt her.

I forget sometimes she's more sensitive than the rest of us.

It's dark driving back, but Eve's face is illuminated by the headlights of the cars traveling in the opposite direction. I turn around and gaze at her and my heart hurts. She's like some dispirited, magical creature that possesses extraordinary powers and doesn't know how to use them. Her parents are sending her to U of K in the fall to study business. Their dream is for her to take over the hardware store when they retire, expanding it into something bigger. A woman with a business degree is unique, according to her parents. She simply dreads the idea. That's her parents' dream, not hers. Her hope for the future is to get lost in New York City, maybe become a famous writer or artist one day. The real heartbreak is that she has the talent to make her mark on the world if given the opportunity. She's an uncut diamond in coal country, and she's miserable. But just for tonight, she's having some fun, and that's about all we can give her.

We're Marie's captive audience for the rest of the ride, forced to listen as she entertains us with her stories of the scattered trail of hearts she's left behind in Richmond. Marie's not planning on going to college. Her family, with all those mouths to feed, doesn't have the money, and her grades certainly wouldn't have helped her anyway. Oh, she's smart, she just never had any interest in what was being taught in school. Her interests are more of a physical nature and using her God-given assets to get what she wants. Her power lies in what you see: a stunning, southern beauty from the Bluegrass. She'll most likely settle down with someone who has money and ambition. Once Eddy's away at college, she'll begin the hunt. She's honest about what she wants— what she needs to do to get what she wants—and she doesn't give a damn what people think. The only person who seems to have a stranglehold on her is Eddy.

It's well past ten when we get back to town and make our way to the river. Audrey turns off the main road and takes the side road that's about a mile or so from our destination. The tires crunch on the gravel. With the windows down I can hear the night sounds, crickets and nature's soft murmurs. The moon's almost full and shining bright. We park in our usual spot. The path to the river is well hidden by the overgrowth of tall grasses and jungle-like brush. It's the best access to the river on foot. I open the door and am greeted with the faint smell of rotten eggs and mother earth, nature's way of saying welcome to the Kentucky River. Though it's dark, the gibbous moon provides us with quite a bit of light. We get out and search through our belongings for the flashlights; we've no intention of building a fire tonight. It's too hot and we certainly don't want to draw any attention. This is our night. Audrey turns her flashlight on and sticks it under her chin. With her face glowing, she makes ghostly sounds. She looks ghoulish, and we laugh. The rest of us shoot our beams at each other, just being silly. Eve's flashlight shines like a floodlight. That thing could land a plane.

"Jeez, Eve, get that thing outta my face. Where'd you even find a flashlight like that?" Marie asks holding an arm across her face to shield her eyes.

"It's an industrial one, we sell 'em at the store," she replies.

"Well, shine it somewhere else, would ya?"

We gather everything from the car and with arms loaded and our flashlights to guide us, we follow the narrow footpath that winds itself down to the river. We know we're fooling ourselves to think that we're the only ones who know about this place, the well-worn foot path is evidence enough. We reach the bottom of the hill, and I can see the outline of the tiny shed several feet away.

"Hey Eve, shine that monster light of yours over here, would ya, so I can see where the hell I'm going and where to put this stuff? Ow, shit!" Marie exclaims.

"What's the matter?" I ask.

"Nothin, just slipped," she says, mumbling a few expletives under her breath.

"Told you, you shouldn't have worn those shoes," I say. She doesn't respond.

It takes us a bit to get ourselves organized. Audrey spreads one of the blankets out a few feet from the shed.

"Best to stay back from the river or we're going to be eaten alive," she says.

"Oh wait, I've got bug spray." I find my bag and locate the can. "Here, I'll use it and then y'all can pass it around." I manage to get a good amount in my mouth and practically choke. "Oh, God, this stuff is awful. Who's next?"

"Here, give it to me," says Audrey who sprays herself down.

Eve places the flashlights in the middle of the blanket, so that their beams shine outward, allowing us to see each other a little better. Besides, it's the closest thing we have to a campfire. We have an up-close view of the river. We can smell it and watch as it sparkles and bounces under the moonlight, gushing and bubbling over rocks along the shallow bank. Marie places the small cooler near the blanket.

"Now for the good stuff," she says. I naturally assume she's talking about what's in the cooler, but she grabs one of the flashlights and makes her way back to the shed. She comes back and plops herself on the blanket, holding a brown paper sack. She reaches in and takes out a bottle. I know without a doubt what it is. I often see it sitting on my own kitchen table. Mama's a fan and one of their best customers. It's what we call "fire water," and it's made right here in the hills, by our most illustrious bootleggers.

"How much you wanna bet that stuff was made only yesterday and in somebody's bathtub?" I say. "You really expect us to drink that? It could probably take paint off a wall."

Marie removes the cap and takes a significant swig. *"WOOOOiiiiieeee!"* She passes the bottle to Eve. "Well, come on, it's time to get this party started." She wipes her mouth and thrusts it at Eve, pressuring her to take a drink.

Cautiously, Eve raises it to her lips and takes a sip. The liquid barely touches her mouth when she begins to spit and gag. We show her no sympathy once again with peals of laughter.

"Here, let me have it," I say. I take a huge gulp, setting my tongue on fire. The hot lava burns its way to my belly. "Oh my God!" I finally catch my breath. "This stuff'll kill ya."

I pass the bottle to Audrey, who tilts it up and takes a healthy swig. There's no physical reaction from her. She just hands it back to Marie and says, "Got any beer in that cooler?" Without hesitation, Marie opens the cooler, pulls out a can, pops the top, and hands it to Audrey. That's more my speed, so I join Audrey. That homemade stuff isn't for me.

Marie produces a pack of cigarettes and lights one. The rest of us decline. Eve finally finds a station on the radio and just for a moment, we are quiet. Just being. Each of us lost in our own thoughts.

"Look over there," Eve says sitting up.

"What are we looking at?" Audrey asks.

"Lightning bugs! There must be a dozen of 'em right over there!"

We watch as they take turns casting their glow, one then another, and still another, each repeating the pattern, like a choreographed ballet.

I break the silence. "You know, they're not called lightning bugs. They're fireflies."

"Where'd you hear that?" asks Marie.

"Oh, I have it on expert authority. Glennis Campbell told me," I chuckle sadly.

"Oh really? Your mama's an authority on lightning bugs, is she?"

"Fireflies," I correct her and continue. "Oh yes, according to Glennis Campbell, lightning bugs are ordinary, nothing special. But if you call them fireflies, now they've become somethin' special, somethin' magical. They're what dreams are made of. Tiny sparks of hope."

"Jesus, Bertie, I never thought your mama would be so daggone inspirational," she laughs.

"Me, neither," I reply.

"Well, then," Marie says standing up and holding her bottle out like she's about to make a toast, gesturing for us to follow. We all stand and raise our drinks. "I, Marie Louise Parker, declare that on this night and from this day forward, we will always and forever be known as the Fireflies of Estill County! What say you?"

"Here, here!" we say, affirming her declaration. We seal it with a clink and a drink.

I've never felt closer to anyone than I do in this moment to these three. I catch the sob in my throat before its escapes. *Oh, how I'm going to miss these girls.* I'm about to tell Marie and Eve our plans when I hear what sounds like a crack of a branch.

"Shhhh... turn the radio down," I whisper.

"What?" Marie asks with her megaphone of a mouth.

"I said be quiet! I think I hear somethin'. Eve, turn that fuckin' radio down!" I command again through clenched teeth. She finally lowers the volume. "Listen."

It's quiet for a few seconds, then there it is again. It's definitely a sound of someone walking on fallen tree branches. "Someone's out there," Audrey says nervously.

"WHO'S THERE?" Marie yells out. Nothing. She yells again, "We know you're out there! Show yourself." We hear his laugh before we see him. We know who it is.

"Eddy, sweetie, what the hell are you doing here?" Marie says. Marie doesn't get scared often, but I can hear the fear in her voice. He's walking toward us—well, staggering. He finally stops several feet away. "Eddy, why aren't you out with Tim and the guys? Thought you'd be out cruising Starlight."

"You, shut the fuck up, Marie! You fuckin' lied to me!" His anger's overflowing, and he's drunk. He steps closer. He's got a small bottle in his hand and takes a swig. He's having a hard time standing still without swaying. He's still wearing the same sleeveless t-shirt and jeans from this afternoon. He plants his feet further apart for support and looks at each of us. "Well, if it ain't the Cher and her cunts show," he says, looking at me. He starts laughing at what he thinks is a hilarious joke. Then he abruptly stops and turns his attention on Eve. "Oh look, it's Tampon, and there's Red, the stuck-up bitch." He steps closer to Eve.

"Eddy, we're just having some fun. I promise, I'll see you tomorrow. Here, I'll walk you back up to your car," says Marie, attempting to put distance between him and Eve. "C'mon babe, come with me." She's using her best sexy kitten performance. The attempt doesn't work. Completely ignoring her, he turns to Eve, makes a vulgar display by grabbing his crotch. "Betcha you've never had this before, have ya? Come 'ere, let me show you what I got for you."

"Eddy, come on, leave her alone," Marie says, pushing him with all the force she can muster. He loses his balance and falls backward.

I move as quickly as I can, grabbing one of the flashlights off the blanket and pulling Eve further away. I don't know what else to do. Audrey grabs a flashlight and moves over to join us. We brace ourselves for what's coming. I know the dangers of dealing with a drunk. It never ends well. I look at Audrey, who's as scared as I am. "Marie, we need to get out of here," I say.

Before Marie can answer, Eddy is up. "You bitch!" he roars, grabbing her by the hair and dragging her like a defenseless ragdoll.

"Eddy, stop! STOP!" she screams as he continues dragging her toward the riverbank.

We run after him, yelling at him to let her go.

"You bitch! I love you and you lie to me! What the fuck, Marie?" He almost sounds like he's crying now. "You think you can play me? You thinkin' maybe you're going to leave me? You're mine, bitch! Do you hear me?"

"Yes, I hear ya, Eddy. Oh, God! Eddy, please I beg ya!!" He rushes her toward the water.

"You're beggin' now, huh, bitch? Look what you're making me do! I'll teach ya to never lie to me again!" He reaches the water's edge and throws her down. She's on her hands and knees, begging him to stop. "Please, Eddy, please, I swear I'll never lie to you again."

Flashlights in hands, we watch in horror as he wraps her hair in his fist and shoves her face under the water.

"Stop, stop, get off her!" I scream. Audrey and I kick and claw at him, desperately trying to get him to stop. I bring the flashlight down on his arm, trying to force him to release her. It doesn't seem to faze him. "Stop, you're going to kill her!" I scream again, grabbing at his hands that are gripping her hair. When that doesn't work, I grab his hair. Still, he seems almost invincible.

He brings her head back up. She's frantically gasping for air, spitting and choking. "You like that, bitch? You want some more?" he snarls. Again, her head goes under. Nothing we're doing is stopping him. It's like he's possessed. Time is standing still; he's going to kill her if we don't do something. She's been under the water too long. The blow comes from out of nowhere, fast and swift, and he releases Marie. We watch in terror as she sinks beneath the surface. Eddy reaches up to the back of his head and to our amazement, rises. *How in God's name is he even standing?* He staggers back several steps, struggling to maintain his balance while still holding the back of his injured head. His face is smeared with river sludge, and his eyes are filled with rage. He's looking straight at me. I move back, my legs almost knee deep in the river, my heart in my throat. He manages to take a single step, then he plunges face first on the bank, his head landing only inches from the water's edge.

"Move, move! Help me, help me! We've got to get her out!" I scream at the others.

She's dead weight, and it's hard to get a grip on her, but between the three of us, we manage to drag her out of the water and onto land. I roll her on her side to release any water that might still be in her lungs. She begins to heave, then throws up. *By the grace of God, she's alive.*

Eddy, however, isn't moving.

Marie begins to catch her breath. She's shaking violently. She's in shock.

"Eve, get a blanket," I say. "Marie, you think you can walk? I know it's hard, honey, but we gotta move, we gotta get outta here. Now!"

"Bertie, you think he's dead?" Audrey asks in terror.

"I dunno, you take her up. I'll be there in a minute," I reply.

Audrey guides trembling Marie up the embankment and meets Eve who wraps a blanket around her shoulders. I turn back to Eddy, who still hasn't moved. I slowly approach him, keeping enough distance between us just in case. I'm afraid to check for a pulse, so I lean down to listen. I don't hear anything. A part of me prays he's alive, the other part hopes he's dead. I'm filled with pure hate and animal fear. *How come there are people like Mama and Eddy in this world? They poison it for everyone.* I'm not sure, but I think he just moved, and I jump back. I need to get out of here, but I will myself to slow down and think. I pick up the flashlight and wash it off in the river.

I do my best to wash away Marie's vomit, using my arms to splash river water over it, hoping I've been successful. I take the next thirty seconds to survey the bank of the river with the flashlight for any items that we might have dropped during the struggle, while the entire time, I'm watching for any movement from Eddy. None so far. When I'm satisfied that I've done what I can to hide any evidence along the shoreline, I give Eddy's lifeless form one last glance, then hightail it up the embankment as fast I can go.

"Is he alive?" Audrey asks with arms full of blankets, dangling the cooler from her wrist.

"I don't know, but we gotta get outta here. Eve, grab what you can and take Marie up to the car. Audrey, you and I gotta get everything out of here. For God's sake, hurry."

We work frantically in the dark, doing our best to hold onto the flashlights while grabbing everything we can possibly see. It doesn't take long before Audrey and I are weighted down but racing up the path as fast as we can with our heavy loads to meet Eve and Marie. Audrey drops her bundle behind the car and fumbles in her bag to locate her keys. The jingling tells me she's found them and is trying to open the trunk.

"Shit, somebody give me some goddamn light, would ya?"

I dump my load and direct the beam of light towards the rear of the car. The light catches Audrey, and she looks like a wild spirit, her face frozen in fear, hair in tangles, and her pale skin almost translucent as she frantically locates the right key, inserting it into the trunk.

"Let's go—let's get it all in there," I command. We begin heaving everything inside.

"Wait! Did anyone get my radio?" asks Eve.

"Hell, I don't know! Quick, let's see!" I shine the flashlight in the trunk and rummage as fast as I can through the bags and blankets. It's not here. *Shit, shit, shit!* "Eve, are you sure you didn't pick it up and haven't dropped it somewhere around the car?" We begin frantically searching the ground around the car's perimeter, but no fucking radio! "Damn it! Maybe it's somewhere along the path or it's still down there somewhere. I'm gonna have to go back," I realize with sobering clarity.

"Leave it," says Audrey.

"Are you kidding? It's evidence…. I'll be right back," I say, turning to leave.

"You know if he's still alive… he's gonna kill you. Eventually, he'll kill all of us. It's not going to be enough for him to make our lives miserable. Believe me, I know what he's capable of," Marie says, defeated.

"Oh, Marie, we know what he's capable of." Audrey states the obvious.

"He's not gonna kill us. Don't talk like that. Get in the car, start the engine, but don't turn on the headlights. Wait for me. I'll be right back." They just stand there, looking at me. "Move, damn it, NOW!" They do.

I am terrified and shaking so badly it takes both hands to keep the flashlight steady as I descend the path, the shaft of light bouncing uncontrollably as I hunt for the radio. I just keep moving. I don't know if he's dead or not; I don't know what to do. I'm sick. I mean, I'm physically sick and feel like I'm going to throw up. I force myself to swallow, to breathe, trying desperately to connect my brain with my feet, one step after the other. *Move, damn it, move your ass.* My heart's throbbing in my chest, pulsating, vibrating through my entire being. I halt halfway down the path and listen. I don't know what I'm expecting to hear, but my actions are involuntary. I don't seem to have control over anything. *Keep moving.* I reach the bottom and turn off the flashlight. If he's alive and managed to survive the blow, he could very well be out there, ready to strike again. I'm unsuccessful finding the radio and step from the path and into the clearing. The night sky's filled with stars. The moon is a shining orb, and I can see the outline of the shed and our little makeshift campsite that only moments ago was our safe place. Again, I stop and listen. I'm not hearing anything but the rush of water from the river, so I turn the flashlight back on and move forward, keeping the beam low. I scan from left to right, hoping the radio is in the general area where we left it. I'm panicking. I don't see it, what are we going to... my foot kicks something, I direct the beam to my feet, and there it is. *Oh, thank God!* I grab the radio and am ready to run outta here when I hear the sound of a large splash. I turn to the river and look.

Present Day

THIRTEEN

It's a little after twelve noon when Dolores's sister, Jane Richards, and her adult son Clayton arrive at the hospital.

Jane's several years younger and several pounds lighter than her sister, but there's no mistaking they're related, because they're wearing the same face. The resemblance is uncanny, and although I've met Jane a few times over the years, I always seem to do a double take when she walks in the room. The dominant brows, the narrowness of the eyes, and the thick, jutting chin all belong to the same set of chromosomes. Not to mention their voices—they sound almost identical too. It was even more apparent yesterday when I had to call her about Dolores's heart attack. If I didn't already know who I was talking to, I would have sworn it was Dolores on the line. Clayton looks to be in his early forties—salt-and-pepper hair, full beard, and a very pleasant demeanor. Sometimes you can just tell when a son is devoted to his mother.

"So, I see you're continuing to *not* take care of yourself," Jane says with little compassion.

"Hi, Aunt Dolores," Clayton greets his aunt with a kiss on the cheek. His beard tickles her face, which she doesn't attempt to hide by wrinkling her nose and scratching her cheek.

"Good God! That beard of yours feels like sandpaper, nephew."

"I see you haven't lost your whimsical side," Jane says, directing her remarks to her sister.

That's all it takes for these two siblings to begin the volley of barbs and verbal jabs. It's almost too much to be in the presence of two Doloreses, so I exchange a few pleasantries with Jane and her nephew and take my leave, assuring Dolores that I'll check back later on today.

Family, ain't they great?

I'm feeling so squirrelly that I practically run to the parking garage, desperate to escape this infirmary. All I want to do is get into a hot shower and let the remnants of these past two days wash down the drain.

I arrive home to a really pissed-off Simone. Her cries of hunger are so relentless, I can't even get my coat off.

"You're being a little dramatic, aren't you?" I ask her.

She answers with—well, let's just say by her vocal feline protests I know what she's saying to me in her native tongue, and I don't appreciate her tone. Not one bit.

I feed the princess to shut her up. I go upstairs to the bathroom and turn on the shower to a temperature that is somewhere between hot and just short of third-degree burns. I strip off everything and get in, letting the water act as my therapist, exposing every single pore, letting it penetrate the skin, and then, without warning, come the tears. I'm in pain, the throbbing pain that comes from having to relive one of the most traumatic days of my life, exposing my truth. Only the day Joe died compares. But reliving what happened that night at the river so many years ago is torture. I was—we were all—so young, we didn't know how to cope with something like that. It was fight or flight. We did both. I lift my face to the shower stream and let the water massage my face. I lather my hair with shampoo, letting the act itself be soothing. I think about what Dolores said when I finished. I was expecting some catty yet clever remark, or a piece of cynicism—her attempt to cauterize the fresh wound I'd ripped open, but that's not what I got. Dolores had tears in her eyes. "I'm so sorry that happened to you."

I made it into the office around three. Beaker was on the phone, so I tapped on Annie's door. "Hi, everything okay?" I ask.

"Yeah, good. All's well."

"What about—?" I nod in the direction of the next room, without asking out loud how things are with Beaker.

"It's fine. He's fine, we're fine," she says.

"That's a lot of fines."

"He's even going to teach the bump," Annie points to her tummy, "to play the guitar."

"Wow, like, right away?"

"No, we thought we'd give him or her a year or two." She stops and looks at me intensely. "Mom, I hope you don't mind me saying this, but you look tired. I know you don't want me to worry, but I do, and I *am*."

I sit down in the chair in front of her desk. "That I am, Annie. I'm not going to lie to you. I'm exhausted. I did manage to get a shower and grab a bite to eat, so I'm good for now. One day at a time, okay? So, tell me what I've missed."

We spent the next several minutes catching up on a few cases. Annie's a brilliant lawyer and she always amazes me, though I know I'm a bit biased when it comes to my daughter. She has quite the reputation as a bright, young star in the legal community. My mind wanders while she's talking. I envision she and Jack as a team. No matter what my previous thoughts have been regarding Jack Hamilton, this baby's going to have one helluva set of parents—a dynamic duo, that's for sure. If I were to make a prediction, Annie will achieve her goal of one day having a seat on the bench. *Judge Annie Meredith Dunnigan*, her middle name chosen in honor of Audrey's middle name. Yes, Judge Dunnigan, I like the sound of that. I just don't want my past to destroy her future.

"And I told him he'd better come up with a better strategy than that if he expects to win his case," Annie says. I nod. I don't have a clue what she's talking about.

"Alright, sounds like you got everything under control." I glance at my watch. "Let me check on a few things and I'll meet you and Beaker in the conference room in, say, fifteen minutes?"

"Sounds good."

I turn on the computer and check emails with reluctance, fearing "Fireflies" will once again find its way to my inbox. I'm granted a reprieve, no further instructions, but several cases come up that need my attention, along with confirmations on my flight, hotel, and rental car reservations for Tuesday evening. I check to make sure I didn't make any errors while I was securing reservations in my zombie-like state, in the dark on a cellphone, punching dates, times, and credit card information in the early morning hours at the hospital. With all that, how could I possibly have made an error? Highly likely indeed. I bring up the flight email. I'm schedule to fly out Tuesday afternoon, landing at Ronald Reagan International just before eight p.m. I've yet to reserve a return flight. I check the rest of the confirmations. I'll pick up the rental car at Hertz and should make it to the hotel by no later than ten p.m. It shouldn't take more than twenty or thirty minutes from the hotel to get to Audrey's house by the following day. I know beyond a shadow of a doubt it's Audrey who's setting up this little rendezvous. She's the only one of us living and working in the DC area, plus, I did a search to see the physical location, the satellite view of the house. One step further gave me the name on the address, Audrey M. and Michael P. Kenton. Audrey's asking for us to meet. Well, I'm assuming the others will be there too. I could be wrong.

Annie interrupts my thoughts. "You ready?"

"Yeah, coming." I grab a legal pad and pen and meet them in the conference room. Beaker, as per usual, is wearing his Bose headphones and strumming on the table. He removes them when I enter.

"Okay, guys, several orders of business I need to update you on. First, I'll be out of town from next Monday afternoon until the end of the week. I can't give you the exact date when I'll be back because I don't know. So, you will have to cover a few things. Tomorrow, I'll meet both of you individually and give you specific instructions. The timing of this makes it doubly difficult, but I wouldn't do it if it weren't important. And, just so you know, this isn't a business trip, this is personal. A dear friend of mine from many years back is asking for me, and I need to go. She lives in Arlington, Virginia."

"Who lives in Arlington? I didn't know you knew anyone from there," Annie says looking surprised.

I think hard about how to approach this. I finally conclude that honesty, in small doses, is going to be the best policy. "No, I've never told you about Audrey. There was a time when we were best friends. I haven't heard from her in years, but it looks like she needs my help. So, I'm going to go see what I can do to help her. I can't really say any more than that right now. I know this is putting a burden on you both, which leads me to my next order of business."

Annie and Beaker look at each other.

"We need to bring in another lawyer. With Dolores out of commission, and our workload growing beyond our capacity, we need help."

"You're not thinking of asking someone to come in as a partner, are you?" Annie asks. Worry is written on her face.

"Nope, I just want someone who's exceptional and looking for a job. Should be easy to find, right?"

"Right," they both say.

"Beaker, you're in charge of doing whatever we need to start the process. Please don't say anything to Dolores yet. I'd like to tell her myself. I'm not in any way replacing her, but the reality is, this little firm is growing, and we need help. Any questions? Nope? Okay, I'm done."

I adjourn the meeting to call the hospital. Jane answers and lets me speak to Dolores.

"Can you come pick me up? This woman's driving me crazy!"

"No can do, kiddo. Why don't you start shouting out racing stats? She's sure to leave the room."

"Good idea."

"I know you don't want me to ask, but how you doin'?"

"I'd be better if they'd stop with all these damn tests. I'm eighty-two years old, for Christ's sakes!"

I hear Jane in the background telling Dolores to stop using profanity.

"Dolores, let them do their job. Isn't that what you always tell our clients? Let us do our job."

"Huh," she says. "You got me there."

"Oh, score one for me. I'll be by to see you tomorrow. You try and calm down—get some rest."

"You can't rest in this place, it's impossible!"

"Well, do what they tell you to do. We want you out of there, too. Love you," I say and I mean it.

"Me too," she says.

"See you tomorrow." I hang up. As hard as it was to share some of my story with Dolores, it does help me feel less alone.

I let Beaker and Annie know how Dolores is doing. Annie comes into my office and closes the door. "I know you don't want to tell me anything right now, but I'm here for you when you're ready. I'm not going to badger you or guilt you into telling me something you're not ready to talk about, but I'm here."

"I know, sweetie."

She stands up to leave, walks behind my chair and wraps her arms around me. "Just for the record, you're a terrific mom," she says.

"Just for the record, you're a pretty terrific daughter."

She closes the door, and I'm left wondering if she'll still feel that way in the very near future.

I think about my own mother. I never got to tell Dolores the rest of the story about that night, about the last time I saw Mama, and the first time she'd ever told me the truth.

1975

FOURTEEN

Estill County, Kentucky

"Go, go, go!" I scream, jumping into the passenger seat and slamming the door. Audrey reacts quickly, shoving the car into drive and pulling out as fast as possible.

"Did, you see him, is he alive?" Marie asks me. The same question everyone keeps asking.

"I don't know."

"What about the radio? Did you get the radio?" Eve says desperately.

"I got it," I say holding it up as proof.

"Should we go to the police?" Eve asks.

"NO!" both Marie and I shout.

"We can't go to the police. They'd never believe us. Eddy's got a cousin who's a cop in Richmond. Eddy's daddy's not one to mess with, either. He'll be out for blood.

Either way, we're fucked. Eddy's protected around here." Marie's words confirm our reality.

"What do we do then? If he's alive, we're sunk. If he's dead, we're done," Audrey says, trying to keep the car on the road.

"I dunno, let me think," I say, my mind racing in a state of panic.

We are all silent. I rack my brain trying to figure out our next move. Audrey breaks the silence. "Where am I going?"

"I don't know. I really don't. Just drive. I'm thinking," I lash out.

"They're going to be looking for him by tomorrow. We've gotta do something fast," Marie pleads.

"Okay, look. Audrey and I were going to tell y'all tonight anyway that we were planning on leaving next week. I had a ticket for Nashville and was going to get one for Audrey." I turn to Audrey. "You know this means we'll have to take the car and get outta here."

"Yeah, I know. We don't have much of a choice, do we?" Audrey asks.

"Marie, Eve, you can come with us if you want. I wish I had a better plan, I really do, but I'm afraid Marie's right. It'll be bad for us if we stay. If we find out later he's alive, then maybe after some time has passed, maybe then, whoever wants to come back can come back."

"I'm not coming back. If he's alive, it *don't* make no difference how much time's passed. He'll be out to kill me; he'll be out to kill all of us. I swear to GOD he will!"

"Then I'm coming, too. There's nothing for me here anyway. No, I'm coming with you," says Eve.

"What about your folks, Eve? Are ya just going to leave and not tell 'em? It'll break their hearts." Marie is genuinely concerned for both Eve and her parents.

"Well, what about you? Any of ya?" Eve says, almost to the point of hysteria. "No, I don't have a choice any more than y'all do. If I were to stay and tell 'em 'bout all this, well, they'll want me to go to the police, and like ya said, that's not really an option. What good's staying if y'all are gone anyway? No, if y'all go, then I'm going, too."

"Are you sure, Eve? Marie? If we do this, there's no turning back," I say and mean it.

Marie and Eve look at each other, then look at me and shake their heads yes.

"Okay, then. Here's what we gotta do." I close my eyes, trying to visualize what comes next. "We're gonna need money, among other things. Audrey, let's head over to my house. You can park down the street a ways, and I'll go in and gather up some of the things I think we'll need. I won't be long. Mama'll most likely be home, but by this time of night she'll either be passed out in front of the television, or close to it. Y'all will stay in the car. We don't want to draw any attention to ourselves, or the car. If for some reason, something happens..."

"Like what?" Eve interrupts.

"I dunno, Eve. Something. Like, maybe a dog barks and someone turns on their porch light and they get suspicious when they see the car. I really don't know, but anything's possible. So," I begin again, "if something should happen and you need to get out of there fast, meet me around the corner of the diner. You know, Audrey, where you parked today before work? If I come out and y'all are gone, I'll meet you there."

"Okay," Audrey says. "You sure you don't want me to come with you?"

"No, it's better I go alone."

"Okay, if you're sure."

"I'm sure."

When we reach the block, Audrey parks the car just down the street and around the corner from my house. Folks have their windows open because of the heat, but I don't see anyone on their porch or moving around outside. Audrey turns off the car's lights but keeps the engine running.

I open the car door, trying to make as little noise as possible. "Okay, I'll be back as soon as I can. Remember what I said," I whisper, "and stay as quiet as you can." They all nod. I push the door silently closed, walking, trying not to run, so I don't draw attention to myself. My house comes into view. I have an unexpected physical and emotional reaction to seeing it. A lump forms in my throat, and I swallow hard. I refuse to cry. This is no time for tears. I keep going, knowing without a doubt that this will be the last time I will ever have to set foot in this house.

I enter through the back, the overhead light in the kitchen's on. The hinges squeak on the screen door; it can't be helped. There's laughing coming from the living room—it's the television. Mama's handbag's sitting open on the table, along with a few pieces of unopened mail and a half-eaten sandwich on a plate. I hesitate for only a moment before I reach into her handbag and remove the small, black change purse she's had for as long as I can remember. I suddenly have flashes of me as a child and her handing me coins from that change purse for an ice cream or penny candy from the five and dime. It makes me sad, but I don't waste any time, nor do I feel one iota of guilt removing what's in it. She's got a couple of ten-dollar bills and a few ones. I take the tens and leave the rest. I tiptoe down the hall. Everything's dark except for the light from the TV. I hear the low hum of Mama's oscillating fan that she keeps on her side table for hot evenings like this. I peek into the living room. She's seated in her chair. Her back is to me, she doesn't see me. There's a cigarette burning in the ashtray, I watch the smoke eerily curl and rise through the air. She lets out a throaty laugh, something amuses her on television. Damn, I really wish she'd been asleep, or more accurately, passed out, but I can't worry about that now.

I take the stairs quickly, hoping the TV and fan will drown out the noise.

As fast as I can, I go to the closet and get the most important thing we'll need, the box with my money. I pull the light cord at the top of the closet and frantically push everything on the floor aside. I get the box out from under the floorboards, checking to make sure the money's still there. It is. Everything's still there. I add the twenty bucks I took from Mama's purse to the booty. There's at least enough money for us to survive for a while. I grab as many clothes as I can off the hangers and scoop up a couple pairs of shoes. I throw everything on the bed, then go back to the closet and get the only piece of luggage I own, a small faded blue case that Mama bought at a yard sale for fifty cents. It doesn't hold much, but it'll have to do. I shove everything in, then begin pulling things out of my drawers—underwear, bras, socks, nightgowns, absolutely anything we can share. I stop for just a second to think. I pull the pillowcase off my pillow and hurry to the bathroom. I begin dumping everything I can into it—in goes my toothbrush, toothpaste, soap, deodorant, shampoo, my hairbrush, sanitary napkins, and even a roll of toilet paper is added to the collection. I'm sure I'm missing something, but I don't have time to take inventory. I go back to the room and make a quick check. *Did I miss anything?* I check the closet one more time.

"Going somewhere?" comes her voice behind me.

I freeze, then slowly turn around. Mama's standing in the door, surprisingly without a drink in hand. Her hair's loose around her shoulders, and she's wearing her favorite flowered robe. "Yeah, I am."

"Far away?" she asks. When I don't answer, she tries again. "Where ya goin'? Oh, don't tell me, let me guess. I'll bet you're heading to that high-falutin' college in Nashville, what's its name again?" Still not getting a response from me, she presses on. "You think I don't know you, Bertie. I do. You know why? Because you're just like me."

I'm surprised she doesn't appear to be all that drunk. But Mama can hold a whole lot of liquor before showing any signs, and then she can turn on a dime. I'm not afraid of her, I was just hoping to get outta here before she saw me and avoid any of this. I can't stop myself and take the bait. "I'm nothing like you."

"Oh, you don't think so, but you are. You are just... like...me...," she says, letting each word drag along for effect.

"I'm not listening to you anymore. I'm getting the hell out of here," I say without affect.

The suitcase is open, the box inside on full display. "Well, I can see you've taken good care of my box for me."

I don't say a word.

She starts to move toward the bed. I step over to the suitcase, close it, and snap it shut. "Oh, I see, it's going to be like that," she says. "Well, how 'bout this? You just give me them pictures, you can keep the rest."

I ignore her and pick up the suitcase and pillowcase. She's still standing in the doorway. "Get outta my way, Mama," I say with force. She's not sure what I'm going to do, so she steps back and lets me pass. I head down the stairs.

"You know, Bertie," she calls after me. "For a smart girl, you're really blind and stupid about some things. You see what you wanna see, not what is. I know what you think, you think that picture you got there's of me and your daddy, don't ya? Well, I hate to break it to ya, Bertie, it's not." Her laugh is cruel, dark, and ugly. "Oh, it's Jesse Campbell, alright, in those pictures, sure enough." I stop halfway down the stairs and turn around to face her.

She's standing on the top step, her hands on her hips, wearing her cruelty like a badge. I want so badly to run up those steps and shove her as hard as I can and watch her fall headfirst to the landing below. But I don't move. I want to hear it. I know what's coming. I need to hear it.

"What are you saying?" My voice quivers, and I can't stop my bottom lip from trembling. I watch her smile grow even wider. She's taking such pleasure in this.

"I'm saying, that ain't a picture of your daddy. In fact, I don't even know your real daddy's name. I met him in a bar one night, up in Lexington, when Jesse was out of town. He was working, riding the trains, leaving me by myself for weeks on end. Who could blame me for being lonely? I was young and pretty and in need of companionship. That night, that young fella gladly obliged me. I don't remember much about him, but I do recall he had real dark hair—that must be where you get yours. I'll tell you this, though." She pauses, then her expression changes, as if something painful just dawned on her. She stares straight ahead before continuing. "Jesse did love you. He used to call me his firefly, but when you came along, you became his little firefly 'cause he said you brought such light into our lives. The first night we brought you home, he was holding you on the front porch when a firefly landed right on top of your blanket. He reached out and caught it before it flew away. He put it in that jar to remember the night you were born." She continues, her voice thick with regret, her eyes focused on the memories of a better place and time. "Yeah, he loved you, he really did, and for a while, we were all real happy. Then that one night changed it all, we got into this terrible fight. He'd been gone too long, and I was so mad at him, I wanted him to hurt like I hurt, so I told him about you. I told him you weren't his firefly. You know what he did, Bertie?" She's choking on her words. "He sat right down there." She points to the bottom of the steps. "And he cried, and he cried, and he cried like a baby. Then he left."

I look at the face of this woman, my mother, and realize that there's nothing else she can do to me. She's delivered her final blow. I'm suddenly so tired I don't know how I'm going to make it down the stairs, let alone carry this load to the car. Turning my back on her, and with the strength I have left, I carry the suitcase and drag the pillowcase down the steps and out the door. I don't look back. As difficult as this night's been, I find solace in knowing that I will never have to lay eyes on her again. I'm relieved when I see the car. The girls are still there, waiting for me. *Thank God I have them—at least I have someone.* Audrey sees me coming and quietly gets out, looking around in either direction to make sure the coast is clear. I gesture for her to stay quiet and open the trunk. I throw everything in and bring the trunk lid down slowly, silently pushing until I hear the click and I know for sure it's closed tight.

We get back in the car the same way, desperately trying not to make a peep.

"Everything okay?" she asks.

"It is now," I reply. Nobody says a word. The car's deathly quiet, but I finally break the silence. "There's been a slight change in plans. We need to go west, head in the direction of Louisville."

Present Day

FIFTEEN

I'm up early and curled on the window seat in the bedroom barefoot, afghan around my shoulders and coffee in hand, as I watch the morning awaken over the rooftops of the houses across the street. There's a Presbyterian church that sits on the adjacent corner just across the way. It's a stone's throw from the house, and the church steeple can be seen clearly from my window. There's something magical, peaceful, and yes, God-like about seeing the sun rise behind the spire. It settles me and I'm appreciative for being privy to its morning routine. I sip my magic elixir and think, wondering what's to come. I have no answers, but after sharing most of my story with Dolores, I believe it might be possible to face whatever's in store. Or could it have the exact opposite effect? By shedding the layers and layers of protection I've spent a lifetime using as insulation, am I now exposing myself to greater risks? I know I'm emotionally drained, so sick of this "thing" that continues to lurk in my subconscious, the "thing" that stands in the way of my living in peace. And now there's a grandchild on the way. I want to be there for that little person, share in his or her life, watch them grow, play peekaboo, and teach them "Itsy-Bitsy Spider" and all those other silly children's games. I hope I can. Simone jumps into my lap and stops me from further wallowing in my pool of self-pity. *Good God, Bertie*, I tell myself. *Enough, quit following yourself down this rabbit hole. It serves no purpose. Get on with it, get on with today.*

"C'mon, lady, let's get you fed and me movin'."

She must comprehend what I'm saying because she leaps off my lap and heads for the door stopping only briefly to glance back to see if I'm coming. Like the trained cat owner I've become, I follow.

Once Simone's fed, I take a five-minute shower, quickly blow-dry my hair, and use the curling iron to try to give it a little something. I'm not sure what that little something is, but at least it appears that I've tried to look like I care. I apply mascara, lip gloss, and a little light blush. I look in the mirror. If there was a before and after photo series of this morning's attempt to fix my face, those pictures would be identical. I breathe in as deeply as I can until my lungs completely fill. I slowly exhale, releasing my breath. My face has grown thinner, and the dark circles under my eyes are becoming more pronounced. I don't look like my mama; Annie does. I don't know who I look like. I don't know who I am. It's a strange feeling not knowing half of yourself, and wishing you weren't the other half either. I've been tempted to do one of those DNA kits where you send a cheek swab and they tell you who you're related to, but I always decide against it, because I'm not sure I really want to know. Plus, that's a sure-fire way for someone to find you if they're looking for you. The case I had last year landed the real perpetrator in jail, exonerating my client for that very reason. We were ecstatic about the results, but it also proved that science can be either your friend or foe. I'm better off not knowing. I wake up from my wandering thoughts and finish getting dressed. I've got too much to do today, and I need to shake off these unwelcome thoughts and get things done.

The last few days have cooperated nicely. The weather's much improved, with temperatures back in the sixties, but I'm not fooled. Things around here can change very quickly. Maybe I can even go for a run in the park tomorrow or take a long walk. Doing something normal would feel good. I start the car and look at my watch. I'm on schedule this morning, so I decide to stop in and see Dolores. I wouldn't be surprised if there's a murder scene when I get there. Either sister could be the victim; either could be the killer. Either way, her motive would be justified. I can't imagine what life was like in their house growing up under the same roof—a battlefield for sure—and if I were a betting lady, I'd lay odds that both sisters won an equal number of battles.

I walk in the room and Jane's in the vinyl recliner leaning back reading a novel. Dolores isn't there.

"So, where's the patient?"

"They whisked her away just a few minutes ago to run a stress test. I told them they should run one on me. I told 'em she's never stressed out. She just stresses everybody else out."

I laughed. "Well, other than what we already know, how is she?"

"Incorrigible. As far as that cold heart of hers, well, the doctor said she dodged a bullet and needs to take better care of herself. No more whiskey, better diet, generally all the common-sense things we already know. We both know she won't listen."

"I know. She's used to living life on her terms. I doubt that's ever going to change. Well, is there anything I can do for you?"

"No thanks, sweetie. My son's gone to Dolores's apartment to shower, and he's bringing back a few things I need. We're fine. The doctor said they're probably keeping her for the next couple of days for observation, mainly because of her age. I'm the lucky one who's gets to tell her."

"Oh boy, well, good luck! Well, I'm going to scoot. Would you tell her I stopped by and that I'll call her later? If you need anything...here, let me give you my cell number." I grab a pen that's sitting on Dolores's hospital tray and write on the corner of the racing form next to her bed. "Take care."

In no time, I reach the office, walking down the bacon-filled hallway, past Beaker who's sitting at his desk in front of his computer, headphones secured to his ears. I give him a wave. I pass Annie's closed door, and I can hear her talking on the phone in her "lawyer" voice—direct, clipped, and to the point. Nothing at all resembling the gushy, giddy girl who announced her pregnancy a few days ago.

I spend the next hour and a half of undisturbed time taking care of as much as I can. Beaker buzzes, letting me know my 10:30's here, the gal I'm defending on the embezzlement charges. After I finish my meeting with her, it's close to lunchtime. I walk out to see Annie putting on her coat. She informs me she's meeting Jack for lunch. Beaker's heading out too; he's picking up lunch and taking it to Dolores. I don't waste my breath, it would be pointless. Looks like I'm holding down the fort, no problem. I go to the front and ask Missy if I can order one of her famous egg salad sandwiches, which she promptly supplies. I take my lunch to the office and spend the rest of the afternoon deep in work. Time gets away from me, and next thing I know, it's late afternoon. My shoulders are sore, so I stand up and stretch. This is a good place to call it a day, and I'd like to run a few errands before going home. I stop by Annie's office and tell her I'll call over the weekend. I say bye to Beaker and head out the door.

My first stop is the drugstore. I need to pick up a prescription along with some travel items. I wander down the aisle, throwing shampoo, body wash, toothpaste, and other toiletries into my basket. I stop—it's déjà vu. I've done this before. I think about the girls and the night we fled. Will I see all of them soon, or only Audrey? I move to the pharmacy counter and pick up my prescription, paying for my other items as well. I'm still thinking about them as I drive in the direction of my house. I pass the library and a sudden idea causes me to slow down, so I turn right, circling the block, and I pull into the parking lot of the library. I enter and scan the area where the public can access the computers. I finally ask the librarian to direct me, and she points me in the right direction. Finding an empty seat at one of the computer stations, I sit down and log on. I haven't done searches on any of them for several years, and never on a computer that can be traced back to me. This might be a good time to see what I can find out. I place my fingers on the keyboard and pause, trying to decide who to begin with, and then start to type in a name. *Audrey M. Kenton, Arlington, Virginia.* I hit search. Two more clicks, and lo and behold, I'm staring into the face of my best friend.

1975

SIXTEEN

Louisville, Kentucky

"You okay, Bertie?" Audrey asks me now that we're on the highway.

"Okay? No. But give me some time, and I will be."

This is the only time I can remember when anything's left us all entirely speechless. We drive. My eyes are fixed on the side mirror, and although it's dark, I watch the last eighteen years of my life unfurl. The tragedy of it all—my life with Mama, Eddy's depravity, not saying goodbye to Billy, and the horrific situation Audrey's in—leaves me numb. I can't feel anything. I don't even have the slightest urge to cry. It might come later, I don't know, but right now, nothing.

Eve breaks the silence. "How long y'all think it'll take for them to come lookin' for us?"

"Depends."

"Depends on what, Marie?" Eve asks, fear in her voice.

"Oh, God, I DON'T KNOW, Eve! How the fuck do I know? I don't know if we killed him, I don't know if he's lying dead or if he's up screaming like some wounded animal, and it's only a matter of time before they start looking for us. I DON'T KNOW!" she screams, letting it all out, her anger and fear raining down on her best friend. Eve recoils from Marie.

Audrey stops her. "Marie, quit screaming at Eve. Just stop! I know you're scared. We're all scared, but screaming and losing our wits doesn't help. Eve, whatever's happened to Eddy, either way, they're going to start looking for us eventually. The best thing we can do right now is to keep moving, use our heads, and for God's sake, stick together. We start turning on each other now, it'll be like rats in a shoebox, as my mama used to say." The mere mention of her mother causes Audrey to stop talking, and a sob escapes. She holds it together the best she can, but I know how badly she's hurting right now.

I continue where she left off. "Audrey's right, we've got to support each other and stay strong, and look out for one another. We're going to make it. I promise we'll be okay. We're smart, we're resourceful, and we can take care of ourselves and each other. I refuse to let anyone, ever again, control my life. Not Mama..."

"Not Eddy," Marie says, following my lead.

"That's right," I say. "Not anybody."

We've only been on the road for an hour and a half, but it feels like forever when we finally make it as far as Louisville. We're all bone tired and decide to find a motel and rest for the night. I suggest we book a place that's in the heart of the city, not a place right off the main highway, no sense making it easy for them find us and besides, the more people and buildings, the less likely we'll draw attention. We can maybe get a little more lost in a crowd, however, with Marie, that can be difficult.

"Marie, I'm going to ask you to keep a low profile. You know what I mean?"

"Yeah, like, maybe keep my mouth shut and my boobs hidden?"

"Well, yeah," I say. "How about we save your charms for when we need them, and I guarantee, you'll get a chance to use 'em."

"Fine, but right now I look like a drowned rat, so I really don't think that's going to be a problem," she says.

None of us are familiar with this city, so we do the best we can trying to find a place to sleep for the night and stay out of sight as much as possible. I don't want to stop and ask for directions anywhere, that's a sure give-away. Finally, I point to an exit that looks promising. It's still right off the highway, which I want to avoid, but it looks like a relatively populated area—lots of buildings, restaurants, gas stations, and motels.

"Let's see where this leads, then maybe we can find a motel that's a bit further from the main road. We don't want to get out so far that we get lost and can't find our way back, but we don't want to be right off the highway either," I say. "Marie, Eve, we're going to need y'all's help too. Keep your eyes open and pay attention to what's around us."

"Okay," Eve says.

"Marie?" I ask just to make sure she's listening.

"Yeah, got it."

We drive another couple of miles and spot what looks like a small hotel just off the road. We're exhausted, and it's after two o'clock in the morning. Audrey turns into the motel's parking lot. There's a neon sign suspended above the entrance: *Vacancy.*

"Oh boy, I sure as hell hope we're not going to catch somethin' sleeping in there. You know what goes on in places like this, and the stuff that's left behind. It's just so gross," Marie says sounding genuinely concerned.

"Marie, we don't have a lot money. We're gonna have to watch every penny for now, so we're gonna have to make do," I tell her.

"You speakin' from experience, Marie?" Audrey teases.

"You bet your sweet ass I am," she says without shame. "So, make sure you sleep on top of *them* covers, unless you wanna take with you somethin' ya didn't bring with ya."

I tell them to stay in the car while I go in and see about a room. The lobby, if you want to call it that, is dimly lit and no one's at the desk.

"Hello," I say, hoping to get someone's attention. "Hello?" I try again. I must be tired because I only now see a small bell sitting to the left of the counter. I ring it several times. For such a little thing, it certainly echoes in this tiny cavern. Finally, I hear someone stirring in the back.

"Coming. I'm coming," says a male voice. An elderly gentleman with a receding hairline is trying to put his glasses on. "May I help you?" he asks. It's obvious I've woken him.

I tell him I need a room for the night. I'm waiting for him to ask questions, see ID, something. He doesn't. He simply says that'll be eighteen dollars and I need you to sign here. I sign it Mary Smith, not very inventive I know, but I'm too exhausted to care. I pay the man in cash and he hands me the key to room 6B. "It's on the backside, so you'll have to pull around." I thank him and leave.

"Well, we're in luck, we've got a room, and it's on the backside, away from the road. Just drive around to the other side."

The room's small—a full-sized bed, a desk, a couple of lamps, and a chair, a TV, and a bathroom with a shower. We're not complaining. We still have the blankets and other supplies that we had with us at the river.

It's hard to believe that this happened only a little over four hours ago. We unload what we need from the trunk and pile it where we can around the room; we're all moving extremely slowly and are wiped out.

"Marie, go in and take a shower. I know you'll feel better," I advise. "We'll make up some pallets on the floor for two of us to sleep, the other two can take the bed."

Eve sits on the bed and begins to quietly weep. I sit next to her and put my arm around her. She lets me hold her as she cries, her tears staining the shoulder of my soiled blouse. Audrey joins us and sits on the other side of Eve. Marie comes out of the bathroom, her hair and body wrapped in a towel. She sits too. The air conditioning unit in the window is blasting semi-cold air and sounds as if it's changing gears. The room smells of cigarette smoke and sex, and yet it doesn't matter, we know we're safer right now than we've been in a long time. Regardless of what's just happened, we need to get some sleep. I insist that Audrey take the bed, and we all agree that Eve will share with her. Marie and I settle into our makeshift bed of blankets on the floor, using rolled-up clothes as pillows. I stare at the ceiling and listen to the erratic sound of the air conditioner trying to perform. I finally fall asleep with visions of the river drifting then receding, drifting then receding, inches from Eddy.

I'm up early and decide to get in the shower before everyone wakes up because I reek. I should have taken a shower last night, but I barely had the energy to make a pallet for myself. I'm stiff from lying on the floor and sit up and listen. There's a chorus of harmonious variations of sleep happening. Marie's the bass, with her deep throaty snores—no surprise there. Eve sound likes a soft train whistle in the distance, while Audrey emits a slow, steady beat. They look so peaceful, and I want to give them more time to enjoy the safety of their slumber. However, I've gotta pee, get cleaned up, and go find us something to eat. I quietly open the suitcase and extract a clean pair of underpants, shorts, and a tank top. I think I've shoved enough in the suitcase for each of us to have at least a change of clothes. We might have to hit a store before we leave and pick up a few things, mainly because I'm not sure Eve can wear anything I brought. It would fall off her.

Audrey's sitting up when I come out. "Hey, you're up early," she says.

"Yeah, I figured I might as well get us something to eat. How ya feeling?"

"Honestly, not great. I've got cramping. It could be from all this," she says, gesturing with her outstretched hand.

"You want me to see if I can find a drugstore or something, maybe get ya some aspirin?"

Her laugh is more painful than cheerful. "I doubt aspirin's going to cure this."

"Guess not. Well, can I borrow the keys and see if I can find us something to eat?"

I tell Audrey I'll be back as soon as I can and that we'll figure out where we go from there. As soon as I step outside, the heat is almost unbearable. It feels like it's close to a hundred degrees today and the concrete under my feet isn't helping. I go the exact same direction we came in, and I'm in luck when I see what looks like a mini mart just at the next light. I get coffees regardless of the temperature because I need it. I place four cups near the register and ask for a carrier, then go and grab a couple of small bottled orange juices out of the refrigerator section and select several doughnuts from the case. I take everything to the counter and the young female clerk begins to ring me up.

"Oh wait! Do y'all carry aspirin?" I ask.

"Yeah, right over there," she answers.

"Can you hold on a moment, please?" I find a bottle of Bayer and bring it back to the counter. I don't know if it will help Audrey—she's right, probably not—but chances are good that one of us is going to need some at some point.

I'm back within a half hour, balancing the coffee carrier in one hand and holding the bag of breakfast in my teeth as I use the other hand to open the motel door.

"Oh, thank God, coffee!" Marie says, taking the tray from my hands.

"And doughnuts and juice," I say, handing the bag to Eve.

"Where's Audrey?" I ask.

"She's in the bathroom. She's been in there awhile. Said she wasn't feeling well," Eve says.

I'm instantly worried. I call through the door and ask her if she's alright. No answer. I open the door a crack, "Audrey, you okay?" she doesn't respond. I go in and close the door.

She's looks up, anguish in her eyes. "I've been bleeding real bad, and I think, I'm pretty sure... no, I know I've just lost it."

Present Day

SEVENTEEN

Audrey still has a beautiful face with those green eyes and that fair complexion, even though it looks as if this web page hasn't been updated for a while. She's aged, like all of us, but there's a calmness about her. That's always been her MO—cool under pressure, showing relatively little emotion regardless of the chaos that's happening around her. I don't think I ever saw her get upset or lose her cool in front of the customers at the diner, come to think of it. Well, except for our last day at the diner when the shit hit the fan with Eddy. The thing that's most shocking is her chosen profession; she's a NICU nurse in a hospital in Georgetown. When she left for Washington, she had dreams of one day being a part of the political scene. She loved politics; she watched the Watergate hearings like they were daytime dramas, which, when I think about it, they were. I don't remember her ever mentioning nursing, but working with newborns, helping to save lives of the most innocent and vulnerable, I can certainly understand the path she took. According to her bio, she's married to her husband of thirty-three years, but there's no mention of any children. My friend seems to have done well for herself, and if anyone deserves happiness, she does.

Up next, Marie. She's always been a bit harder to keep track of, mainly because of her multiple marriages. I worry about Marie more than the others as a potential weak link, not because she would ever intentionally do anything to expose us, but because I've seen enough failed relationships in my career to know that people can be incredibly vindictive, and an angry spouse or partner can do serious damage. Though we swore we'd never say or do anything that would put each other at risk, the truth is (and I've seen it so often), the years pass, people let their guard down, and secrets are shared. I'm guilty of confiding in Joe, and I can almost bet Audrey has shared things with her husband too. I can only hope that with the passage of time, Marie's ex-husbands will keep whatever she might have shared with them in confidence. I've never worried about Eve, she's not a talker.

I begin my search for Marie by Googling the last name I had for her, hoping it hasn't changed for the fourth time. It looks like she indeed stopped on husband number three after all. I find her on Facebook—Marie Tilden, there she is. Owner and operator of Can You Feel It? Beauty & Spa, Fresno, California. What a perfect fit for Marie. According to the post, she's owned and operated this full-service spa since 2012. Her establishment offers facials, pedicures, manicures, and massages, and has a licensed esthetician on staff, whatever that is. I have on numerous occasions indulged in a manicure, but not any of the other services she provides. I've never been interested in the other stuff. In fact, Annie has tried for years to get me to go for a massage. I just can't, it just seems icky to me—one of my many peculiarities, I know. But it appears Marie has made quite a career for her herself, and from her picture, she uses her own services regularly. She's meticulously put together. Her hair is platinum now, long and straight. Those bouncy, beautiful blond curls that once framed that perky face are gone. She's still a pretty lady, just a bit on the synthetic side. I oughta be ashamed of myself, trying to remember the last time I saw the inside of a salon. It wouldn't hurt for me to clean up a bit. I spend a few more minutes on her page, then check a couple of other sites where she's showcased online. Marie is now married to a guy by the name of Owen Tilden, who's in commercial real estate in Fresno. I can find no mention anywhere about her possible children either. That seems strange that neither Marie nor Audrey appear to have had children. Then again, people don't always advertise everything about themselves on social media. The Tildens are obviously well known in their community— numerous pictures are posted of the couple attending sports events, cocktail parties, benefits, and other social events around Fresno. Marie's obviously not afraid to be seen. But then again, isn't that the best way to hide? Just like what I have done, live out in the open.

I leave Eve for last, mainly because I already know quite a bit about her, being our most famous recluse, having written more than a dozen *New York Times* best-sellers under a couple pen names I'm aware of. Unlike the rest of us, Eve never kept her original name, and had it legally changed as soon as she was able to. I think I've read every one of her books, marveling at her brilliance and creative power. Even today I'm amazed that this genius is the same little girl who stood in the corner of that church meeting hall, humiliated beyond belief by those who weren't deserving enough to be seen in the presence of her grace. Eve found her place in New York. I scour the net and find the most recent article, a rare interview with E.M. Donald. I smile because I'm pretty sure she's used the first initials of her name and her mother's name (Eve and Mildred) and taken her father's name (Donald) as her last name. Eve's still in New York, living in Chelsea with her longtime partner, the famous sculptress, Jacqueline C. Monroe. In the back of my mind, I always wondered if maybe Eve was more flattered by the attention she got from that fella at the bar rather than genuinely interested in him—or any fella for that matter.

I sit back and feel such admiration for these ladies, these extraordinary women who have fought insurmountable odds just to be, to exist, under such incredible circumstances. I'm angry—angry that instead of shouting their courage and spirit from the rooftops, they're made—no, *we're* made—to hide our true selves. I wish to Christ we'd been able to be there for each other all these years, but if we'd stayed together, well, let's just say things would have been a hell of lot different for all of us, I'm sure. To this day, I'm still amazed how relatively easy it was for us to slip into obscurity in 1975. How a little bit of ingenuity and tenacity changed the past and paved the way for the future. We did what we had to back then, and there was no Internet to make it as easy as it would be to track us down today. And that's the thing that worries me, too. If someone was actively looking for us now, we would be easy to find.

But I'm still worried about the reason for Audrey reaching out and what the outcome might be. I miss my friends and secretly hope they'll be there. Each of us, whether we want to admit it or not, are who we are because of the lives we lived in Estill County.

Fatigue sets in, and I just can't make myself do any more today, and I log off the computer. It would be nice to go home and decompress a bit. Tomorrow night's dinner with Annie and Jack—that oughta be interesting. If I can just remember that he's not the enemy, I should be fine. Annie's right, I need to give him a chance, get to know him better. I'm always too quick to judge—it's my nature, and an occupational hazard.

I wonder how Dolores is doing. I call her on the way home and check in. She tells me that the doctors are confident that she'll be released sometime over the weekend, though she says yesterday was better for her. Jane will be staying at her place for a couple of weeks; her nephew will fly back to Detroit once she's released from the hospital. At some stage of the game, I'm going to have to tell her we're looking to add another attorney to the mix, and she'll think I'm replacing her. But I really don't have a choice—we're growing and need the help. Dolores can continue to be as involved as she wants, but truth be told, we both know it's getting more difficult for her, and if I'm honest with myself, it has for a while now. There's just so much to think about. I'm ready for a glass of wine and a frozen entrée of baked chicken and

Simone will have the Fancy Feast. Hers will be served à la tin can, mine, superbly prepared in the microwave.

Saturday brings lots of sunshine and lifts my spirits. I take advantage of the weather by enjoying a run in the park. It's the most relaxing thing I've done for myself all week. Normally I get in a good walk or run at least three days a week, but this week I've had to forgo my usual routine. Today it feels good to sweat, and I climb the hills of Cherokee, pushing myself until my lungs burn, not stopping until I literally can't go any further. I slowly wind down until I'm at a walk, gradually cooling my body down, hydrating along the way. It feels good. Lots of people are taking advantage of the weather—cyclists are out in full force, couples running together, mamas and daddies pushing little ones in strollers, and quite an array of dogs keeping pace with their owners. People out living their best lives. I will do everything in my power to do the same. I spend the rest of the day doing things around the house that I have neglected, those mundane chores of laundry, vacuuming, and dusting. I even go so far as to contact a few remodelers, setting up appointments in the next couple weeks for them to come out. The kitchen's way overdue for an update, along with a few other areas of the house. I think it's time to focus on things to come. This might help move me in a more positive direction. It can't hurt. The day's gone before I know it. I've got an hour and a half before I meet Annie and Jack for dinner. I'm going to attempt to make this a pleasant evening because Annie wants so much for me to like Jack. It's simply hard to switch gears when his career has been made by fighting me on all fronts for the past few years. *Damn, why did she have to go and get herself involved with a prosecutor?* Nope, I tell myself not to go there and focus on what to wear. I decide on my pale blue chiffon blouse and a pair of black fitted ankle pants with simple black heels. I wear my hair down, styling it so that it has more volume and falls in soft waves above my shoulders. I've thought about cutting it short, but I always talk myself out of it. I slide on my silver bracelet and finish the look with a pair of silver hoop earrings. I think it's a smart look, yet it softens me a bit. I've been told my appearance can sometimes be rather austere. I've probably done it on purpose, subconsciously keeping people at a distance, wearing an invisible sign that reads *approach with caution*. Tonight, I'm going to try a bit harder. Though today was lovely, nights are still chilly, so I grab my coat before I leave.

By the time I arrive at the restaurant, Annie and Jack are already there, and the hostess escorts me to their table. I notice immediately how radiant Annie looks, and how happy they seem to be together. It's shocking to see what a striking couple they make. My sudden thought is, *My God, this baby will be beautiful.*

Jack rises as I approach and pulls the chair out for me. "Good evening, Bertie. So glad you could join us. I'm sorry... can I call you Bertie?"

"You just did," I reply. "And yes, please do."

"Mom, you look fantastic! *Très chic!*"

"Well, thank you, I was just thinking the same thing about you."

"You both look lovely," Jack chimes in.

I don't react. I don't know why, but for some reason it irritates me. I feel like I'm being played, and I don't like it. I stop myself from saying something derogatory, so I force a smile and say, "Thank you."

"Mom, we really do appreciate you having dinner with us tonight. Jack and I are thrilled about the baby, and of course, scared to death."

"Yes, we're very excited and couldn't be happier. My folks are going to be grandparents for the first time as well, and my mom and dad absolutely adore Annie."

I'm about to ask him more about his parents when we're interrupted by the waiter. He takes our drink orders, and I ask for a glass of Pinot Noir. Jack orders Woodford on the rocks, and poor Annie gets to sip her seltzer water and watch us indulge.

"So, where were we? Oh, you were telling me your parents are thrilled about news of the baby. Annie, I don't remember you mentioning that you've met them," I say, more as a question than a statement.

"Oh, well," she hesitates and sputters a bit. I suspect she's kept that from me intentionally, thinking it might hurt me to know there's an already established relationship with Jack's parents. I'm not upset with her; I'm upset with me. I feel rather ashamed for putting her in a situation where she didn't feel she could be forthcoming.

"Well, if they're half as thrilled as I am, that baby's going to have lots of love and support."

Our drinks come and I raise my glass. "Here's to the both of you and to our new addition."

The smiles on their faces are genuine. *He makes my daughter happy, what more can I ask for?*

The rest of the evening goes well. I even find myself laughing and sharing court stories.

I learn that Jack graduated at the top of his class at Stanford and served as president of his law review. He's ambitious, smart, and appears to love my daughter. He's an avid swimmer and skier and spends his time in Aspen and Tahoe when he can. He becomes animated when talking about skiing and vows he'll teach his child to ski early.

"Well then, we just might have an Olympian in our family," I say laughing.

We're having a lovely evening, and I'm feeling better knowing that these two seem to be a good fit. The meal was delicious, and I order coffee afterwards. When the waiter presents us with the dessert menu, I talk Annie into sharing crème brûlée with me.

"So, tell me, Bertie, where are you from originally?"

The question takes me by surprise, so I reach for my water glass and take several sips before answering, hoping I don't appear rattled. I decide honesty with just a touch of vagueness might work.

"I was born in a small area of Eastern Kentucky, but I've lived in Louisville practically my whole life. How 'bout you and your family? Are you originally from Louisville?" I'm hoping to move the conversation in another direction by not allowing him to ask a follow-up. Annie knows I don't like to talk about my past because it was a painful one. She's always just sort of let it go.

"Yep, all my life. I love this town. It's been good to me. I've been offered jobs in other cities, but I like it where I am."

"It is a great city, isn't it?" I simply say.

When my coffee cup's empty and the crème brûlée is polished off, I tell them it's been a lovely evening and begin to excuse myself. Annie stops me.

"Mom, before you go, Jack and I want to tell you something."

Oh God, she's going to tell me she's getting married. What I'm most worried about with this whole arrangement is the fact that Jack is a prosecutor. If he were ever to find out about what happened in my past, well, I don't want to even think about it. And it's not even about me at that point. I just don't want to see Annie hurt.

"Well, Jack and I have decided to move in together. We're going to sell our condos and find a house together. It's not just because of the baby—well, maybe a lot of it is—but we'd even discussed the idea before I became pregnant. And besides, we want the baby to have a real home." She pauses and eyes me for a reaction. "So, what do you think?"

I look at both of their faces, they're genuinely eager to get my response. "I think if this is what the both of you want, then you should do it," I say.

"I love your daughter, Bertie, I really do, and I'm excited at the prospect of us sharing our lives," he says, reaching over and taking Annie's hands in his own. "I'm excited about the baby coming, becoming a father. I respect you immensely, I really do, regardless if we find ourselves at times as adversaries. And I know how much Annie loves and respects you, too. It was important for us to know that you're on board."

"Of course I'm on board! I want nothing more than to see my daughter happy," I say to him directly. "I promise I'll do everything I can to support the both of you. Be patient with me, though, it's going to take me a while to wrap my brain around this 'grandma' thing." I laugh.

I drive home feeling some contentment. Annie has someone she can depend on, who loves her. I had that with Joe, and there's nothing worse than feeling alone in the world.

When I walk through the door, Simone's curled up on the sofa and barely looks my way. I skip any conversation and walk into the kitchen, flipping on the overhead light. I throw my coat on the chair and take a moment to look around the room. Yes, I'm glad this room's going to get a bit of a facelift. I'm still a bit buzzed from the coffee I had at the restaurant, so I grab the remnants of the Kendall Jackson that's still in the fridge and get a glass off the shelf. I don't bother getting a real wine glass, tastes the same either way, and I don't have to impress anybody tonight. I turn the kitchen light out, and I stop at the bottom of the stairs to kick off my heels. *Oh, dear Lord, does that feel good.* I set the bottle and the glass on my dresser, and just for a moment, I think of Mama. I dismiss that immediately and go into the bathroom to wash my face, changing into my freshly laundered nightgown and my fluffy white robe. I turn on the small lamp on the nightstand so that there's only a soft glow. I return to the dresser and pour myself some of the wine, and then acting on behalf of some other force, I reach in and bring out the tin box. I never did answer Dolores when she asked about it in the hospital. I guess Mama will always be a painful subject, yet I still hang on to this box. I sit at the window seat, realizing I've come full circle, ending the day as it began, except now I'm sipping wine. I remove the lid of the box and hold up the single firefly in the jar. Audrey's face appears in my head.

1975

EIGHTEEN

Louisville, Kentucky

I help her to the bed so she can lie down. Though I've tried to reason with her, she's adamant about not going to a hospital. I'm worried. She's lost a fair amount of blood and looks pale.

I call for the others to help me get Audrey to the bed from the bathroom. Marie's at Audrey's side immediately, helping guide her to the bed. Eve pulls the covers down, but the expression on her face is, without question, complete fear. We get Audrey settled under the covers. She tells me the cramping has subsided and that she just wants to rest for a while.

"Audrey, here, take two of these," I say, handing her two aspirin and a glass of water. I know it's a fucking futile thing to do, but it makes me feel like I'm doing something to help. "Is there anything I can get for you? Are you sure you don't want to go to the hospital?" I try once again. She shakes her head no.

Marie, who's been unusually quiet through this, finally breaks her silence. "Would someone tell me what the hell's going on?"

I ignore her and sit next to Audrey. She's lying on her side, knees drawn into a fetal position. I place my hand on her shoulder and lean close to whisper in her ear. "Audrey, we're here for you, and we're all in this together. They'll want to help. I think we need to tell them. Can I do that—can I tell them? It's entirely up to you." She simply nods. "Okay, you rest. We'll step outside for a minute, and we'll be right back.

The news of Audrey's lost pregnancy and who was responsible hits them both hard, but Marie is livid. She's already planning ways to kill Audrey's father, and they're all slow and painful.

"That's not helping, Marie. We're going to have stay here for a little while longer, just until Audrey feels well enough to go. In the meantime, we gotta make the best of the situation. I'm going to extend the room for a couple more days."

I send Marie and Eve to the store with twenty bucks to get the things Audrey's going to need. When they return, they've bought a deck of cards, along with the other items on the list. We spend the rest of the day and into the night playing rummy and watching over Audrey. We keep the television on, especially in the event that something comes across the news. So far, nothing.

By Sunday morning, Audrey's feeling a little better. Her bleeding has slowed down, and she doesn't appear to have any fever. I'm concerned that money will run out soon. We need a plan. I look over at Eve. Her hair's uncombed and my clothes are two sizes too big on her small frame. She looks twelve years old rather than eighteen. She's just staring straight ahead at nothing—eyes glassy, trance-like. As I watch her, it suddenly occurs to me that Eve just might be our ticket out of this mess. It's risky, but we're going to have to take some chances.

"Eve, you alright?" I ask. "You miss them, don't ya?" She knows immediately I'm speaking of her parents.

"I do. You know, it's funny, I love 'em, I really do, but I was dying a little bit each day. I felt like I was suffocating, and the whole time they thought they were doing the right thing." She looks down, almost choking up.

"Yeah, but at least they care. They really do love you. You have that," I say.

"I guess," she sniffs. "But love's a funny thing, it can work for you or against you."

"I guess you're right. But what if there's a way we can get it to work for us?"

She looks up at me, suddenly attentive. "I'm listening."

All eyes are on me now and I share my idea. I particularly watch Eve's face as I map out this possible solution. It's risky, and it may expose us, but we're going to run out of money soon. I ask each person to tell me their thoughts, pros and cons. We talk about worst-case scenarios, coming up with what to do if everything goes south.

"If anybody has a better idea, let's hear it," I say.

Audrey's sitting up in bed now and has a little more color in her face. "It's worth a try," she says quietly.

"I think it's a hell of an idea. Eve, they'd do just about anything for you, I bet," Marie says confidently. "They wouldn't turn you in, Eve. They just wouldn't."

"I think we're going to have to chance it. First and foremost, we're not sure what's going on back home. This way we'll find out more, but we know there's an element of risk involved. Eve, how do you think they'll react?" I am excited about the idea, but I'm also trying to be sensitive to the fact that we are asking her to do something difficult.

Eve's quiet for a moment. "It depends on who answers the phone. If Mom answers, I have a better chance of appealing to her emotional side. If Dad answers, well, it might be a harder sell."

"So, if your Dad's first to pick up, you hang up. We wait until the next day and try again. What do y'all think?"

"Well, it's sure a hell of a lot better than sitting in this room looking at these stupid four walls. I'm so bored I'm about to lose my ever-lovin' mind. It's time to go!" Marie's all in.

"Eve, I want you to be sure you're okay with this," I repeat, cognizant of her inability to say no at times.

"How can it hurt, Bertie? I'm going to have to trust them to do what they think is right. I'm ready. Let's do it."

"Okay, then." I jump into gear. "Audrey, will you be okay for a bit? We shouldn't be gone too long, just long enough to find out where money can be wired around here. Once we know that, we can make the call."

"I'll be fine... I'm not bleeding so much now. Good luck, Eve! And sweetie, thanks for doing this for all of us. I know this can't be easy."

I drive to the mini mart that's already become our home away from home. I tell Eve to stay in the car while Marie and I go in. We're in luck! There's a pimply faced kid about our age, maybe a year or two older, working the counter. I grab a pack of Juicy Fruit and throw it on the counter, and then I turn to Marie and nod. It's time for her to use her charms. Before I'm even out the door, she's got his full attention. It takes her all of thirty seconds to come out of the place wearing a smile on her face. "Oh my, that was just too easy! I felt like a kitten playin' with a moth. He'll keep his mouth shut. I promise. Here's everything we need." She hands me a piece of paper with an address for the closest Western Union and a phone number, along with two Milky Ways and a Three Musketeers bar.

"Did you pay for those, Marie?" I ask.

"What do ya think?" She bites into her chocolate bar.

We find a phone booth on the outside corner of a liquor store. I've brought change. Eve's nervous, but she steps in to make the call. She keeps the door open so that Marie and I can hear, just in case the conversation takes a turn and she might need our guidance. The coins clink as they enter the phone.

Gripping the receiver in both hands, it only takes a few seconds before she starts talking. "Mom, it's me. Before you say anything, just tell me if there's anyone there besides Daddy?.... Okay, good... Mom, don't cry, please. If you do, I'll hang up." Even standing a foot away, I can hear the panic in Mildred Henderson's voice coming through the receiver as she begs Eve not to hang up on her.

I feel sick. Her parents are most assuredly beside themselves. Eve's quiet. For a full minute, she's just listening.

"Mom, Daddy, I'm sorry if I've hurt you, but I'm not coming back. You can either help me or not, but I wanted you to know that I'm okay. I just need to live my life. You've been good to me, and I appreciate everything you've done. I truly do. But I mean it when I say I want—no, I need—to live my life my way. I hope one day you'll understand, I really do.... No, Daddy! I'm not being held against my will. No, I'm fine. I'm really fine."

I've now figured out that Mr. Henderson is on the other extension and that they're doubling the pressure on her. I could kick myself for not thinking that might happen.

Eve once again stops talking and listens. "They did? .... He is?" She wraps her hand around the cord as if she's hanging on for dear life. "When? Who found....? Sheriff Malone is? Wait, what'd you say? Oh, God. No, I can't tell you that. I'm sorry." Eve begins to cry softly, whatever's been said on the line unnerves her. "No, I can't tell you that. They're my friends, we did nothing wrong.... No, I don't want you to come and get me. What I want is for you to send me some money. I understand if you don't want to, I really do, but if you love me, you'll do this. Please, I'm begging you both. I promise I'll call you and let you know where I am as soon as I can. But for now, I'm safe. Please don't tell them anything. I beg you, but please, please, I need your help now." Eve's forehead is now resting against the glass booth. I can hear their anxious voices on the other end, but I can't make out what's being said. After what seems like forever, Eve whispers, "Thank you." She holds her hand out to me, signaling she needs the address of the Western Union. She repeats it twice, then tells them she loves them and that she'll contact them soon. Then she hangs up. She's drained, so I help her out of the booth.

"They'll do it, but he's dead. He was found this morning floating down river, and the sheriff's looking for us."

"Oh, God! Wait, down river, how's that possible?" Marie exclaims.

"I don't know," I say and head for the car.

Present Day

NINETEEN

I drain my glass, put the box back in the dresser, and get ready for bed, hoping that sleep will come tonight. I turn off the lamp and crawl under the covers, pulling them up to my chin, holding the blankets tight in both hands, like a child who's afraid of the monster under the bed. I hear Simone's soft meow as she enters the darkened room and quietly leaps onto the other side of the bed. I can feel her tiny paws as they make their way across the coverlet to the pillow next to me. She's decided to let me share her bed tonight, I guess. She purrs softly, circling the space, and begins her kneading ritual. Someone told me once that adult cats knead on soft things when they're happy and content, associating it with the time they were kittens being nourished by their mamas. That's what mamas and, yes, daddies are supposed to do—nourish, protect, support, and love their children. In my own life, and in what I've witnessed throughout the years, what should be the natural thing to do as a parent simply *isn't* for some people. I close my eyes and listen to the sounds around me, trying to clear my mind of impending events. I tell myself that all I have is this moment, this space, this time. And although I don't know what the future holds, right now I'm okay. I fall asleep to Simone's lullaby, the gentle rhythm of a kitten's beating heart.

I stay in my pajamas until almost noon. It feels good not to be in such a hurry, enjoying cups of coffee and the Sunday paper. Annie laughs at me for still getting the newspaper delivered, but I can't help it. It comforts me because it's routine, and I have a hard time curling up with my phone and a cup of coffee. I feel physically better today, having finally gotten a decent night's sleep, and I'm thankful for that. I'm going to need to be good and rested for the days ahead. My flight doesn't take off until later tomorrow afternoon, so my plan is to leave from the office and go straight to the airport. I'll have to pack tonight and have my suitcase ready to put in the car in the morning. There's been no further texts or emails from Audrey, so unless I hear otherwise, I will assume it's still a go. A part of me worries it's some sort of trap, but whether it is or whether it isn't, I'm going either way. My thoughts are interrupted by my phone. I don't recognize the number, but I hesitantly answer anyway.

"Hello?"

"Hi, it's Jane." I have a sudden rush of relief. "Just wanted you to know they're releasing Her Highness, and we should have her back at home sometime this afternoon." She pauses. "Can you wait just a minute?" She sounds exasperated.

"Sure." I'm surprised by her abruptness.

"No, I'm sorry, Bertie. I'm not talking to you; I'm talking to Dolores. She's in the bathroom barking orders at me from behind the closed door. Sorry, hold on again. What is it you're asking? ... Yes, she's still on the line. I'm sure she'll wait to talk to you... No, I'm not going to hang up! Wash your hands before you come out of there, or you're going to kill us all. Hold on, Bertie. I've got to help her to the bed."

"Absolutely, I'll wait." I smile picturing these two in my head.

"I guess she told you I'm bustin' out of here today," Dolores says a bit breathless.

"Yes, that's great news. How ya feeling?"

"I'm okay. I'll be better when I can get outta here. How about you? How are you doing?" She takes a more serious tone.

"I'm good, I am. I fly out tomorrow afternoon, and we'll see what happens. But please don't worry. I'll be fine."

"I know you will. I hate to ask, I know you're pressed for time, but would you mind stopping by my apartment tonight or tomorrow before you leave? It'll only take a few minutes—just a couple things I want to touch base with you about."

"Absolutely!" I agree, although I'm rather surprised at her request. I was planning on stopping by anyway before I left. "Wait, Dolores, is something wrong? Is there something you're not telling me?"

"My God, all the questions, I simply asked you to stop by," she bristles.

"Okay, don't get your panties in a wad, lady, I was only asking. I think you should rest tonight. I'll stop by at lunchtime tomorrow, maybe bring you something."

"Ask Missy or Patrick to fix me a cheeseburger with pickles, onions, ketchup, and mustard. Fries on the side and have them throw in a piece of that lemon meringue pie while they're at it."

"Seriously?"

"As serious as a heart attack."

"Very funny. I'll see you tomorrow. You get some rest and behave for Jane."

"Fat chance. Don't forget my cheeseburger," she says and hangs up.

She's impossible. I love her, but she's a real pain in the ass—that's for sure. I get up and make myself get in the shower and get dressed, throwing on a sweatshirt and jeans and my tennis shoes. The sun is fighting hard to shine, but the clouds are winning, I'm afraid. So be it. I grab my jacket and decide to take a walk. I stop and talk to my neighbor across the street, she's out pulling her girls in the wagon. Celia's three and Olivia's almost six. They're darling little girls who are a joy to be around. This past Christmas I invited them over to the house for hot chocolate and to help decorate my famous sugar cookies. Most of the icing landed in their little mouths instead of on the cut-out stars, Santas, reindeers, and candy canes. I was still sweeping up colored sprinkles long after New Year's. It was always a tradition that Annie and I enjoyed doing together—the magic of something as simple as frosting and decorating cookies.

I continue walking down my block, enjoying the beauty of the neighborhood, and appreciating its history. What I wouldn't give to be a witness to its early years, the vibrancy of the area, the Victorian beauties newly built, with families moving in, everything fresh and new and exciting. I'll bet it was something, because it's still something special. It's been a great place to raise Annie and call home.

I turn down the next block and walk the strip, soaking in the energy, which is busy, even for a Sunday afternoon. I move at a leisurely pace, only stopping for the lights to change on the busier streets. I'm thinking, do I want to maybe stop for an ice coffee—when I spy the ice cream shop on the corner. It takes all of five minutes for me to be walking out with a double scoop of butter pecan in a sugar cone. Stress and anxiety normally cause me to lose my appetite, but seldom am I able to ignore ice cream, no matter the situation. I don't have many addictions, but ice cream is without a doubt one of them—well, ice cream, coffee, and dark chocolate, those three things for sure. I'd suggest putting all three together as an ice cream flavor, but I'm not a fan of coffee-flavored anything except coffee-flavored coffee. I'm a purist in that way. I continue on my stroll and eventually take one of the side streets that leads to Cherokee Triangle, circling where once stood the statue of John B. Castleman mounted on his horse, a Confederate officer during the Civil War. Before it was finally removed, I remember seeing it splattered with orange paint, reminding us of our stained past and what those monuments were meant to represent. I loop around the rest of the block, taking my time, seizing the day. My pocket begins to vibrate—I've had my phone on silent, hoping to unplug for a bit. I check and it's Annie.

"Hi, what are you up to?" I ask, licking the ice cream that's melting on my hand.

"Jack and I have been spending the day going to open houses. We've hit three so far, you know, just starting to look around and see what's available and which areas would work best. We literally looked at a house around the corner from you. It's a beauty—charming, lots of potential, but needs some work."

"Any house you look at around here's most likely going to need some upkeep. Piece of advice: charm is great, but how old's the furnace, the air conditioning, the water heater, the plumbing, the roof...? Let me see, what else? Oh yes, the fireplaces, windows..."

Annie laughs. "I get the message. But I love the area! It's where I grew up."

I stop walking and though she doesn't know it, her words have touched a chord in me. I was able to give her something I didn't have. I must have done something right. "It's a special place, a wonderful neighborhood. You sure Jack would want to live so close to the dragon lady, though?"

"I don't know, let me ask him," she jokes. "Yep, he says he's good."

"Really, well, it sounds like you two aren't letting grass grow. Already looking for houses, wow!"

"We only have a little over six months before this baby arrives, and few free weekends between the two of us. So, we're going to do our best to get things done. Hey, where are you, anyway? We stopped by. You obviously aren't home but your car's out front. That's really why

I was calling. Just checking to make sure everything's okay."

"Yes, thanks, honey, for checking on this old gal. I'm just out for a walk, and if you must know, I'm walking and eating an ice cream cone as we speak."

"Oh, no fair, not butter pecan?" It's both our favorite.

"Yep, you betcha!" I laugh.

"Jack, we're going to have to make a stop before going home," she says to Jack. "Okay, Mom... Oh, wait, have you heard from Dolores? How's she doing?"

I spend the next two minutes giving her an update. I tell her I'm going to visit her tomorrow and bring her lunch. Annie laughs at Dolores's lunch request. "Love you, thanks for checking on me."

"Love you too, see you tomorrow, Mom."

I finish the rest of my cone and take my time wandering back to the house. I wonder what it would be like to have my grandchild just around the corner. I'd love that.

I spend the rest of the afternoon and evening doing a bit of necessary work. I'm not sure how long I'll be gone. It could be a day or two, it could be more. There's absolutely no way of knowing until I get there and find out what's in store. Anyway, I try and tie up loose ends. I can finish the rest tomorrow when I'm in the office. Later in the evening, I make a small plate of angel hair pasta and toss it with a little olive oil and fresh parmesan. I don't even want to think about what my food choices today have done to my cholesterol levels. I put together a salad just to minimize my guilt. I grab my plate and a handful of cat treats and make my way to the couch. I toss a few treats to Simone so that I might eat in peace, then turn on the television, find a movie on Netflix, and eat my dinner. I spend the next two hours lost in the most unbelievable story imaginable, but who cares? It's entertaining and takes my mind off things. By ten o'clock I rinse my dishes and turn out the downstairs lights. I go up and do what I've been putting off all day, packing. I check the weather for the Washington, DC, area and find it's supposed to be sunny, but cooler than Louisville. I cram what I can into my carry-on: a couple pairs of lightweight slacks, a pullover sweater, and a couple of blouses. I'll wear some layers tomorrow, that way I'll have some extra and I won't have to pack so much. I finish up and double-check everything, just to make sure I have what I need. I'm ready, I think.

I don't sleep well. I think I might have slept three, maybe four hours at most. I tossed and turned so much that at some point, even Simone relocated. It's 5:30 a.m. and I finally give up and get up. There's nothing worse than trying to make yourself go to back to sleep when you know it's just not happening. I go downstairs and brew myself a cup of coffee, empty the dishwasher, take out the trash (though it's minimal), and water the plants. Before I left the office on Friday, I asked Beaker about taking care of Simone. He said he would, that he'd just stay at the house if I wanted. I could've kissed him right then and there for making my life easier, but it's Beaker and he's not a fan of public displays of affection. I do wonder how he's doing. Is he sad, or angry, or hurt? Maybe all of the above regarding Annie and the change in her relationship status and her new starring role as mother to be? Beaker's a hard one to read, but the best damn law clerk I could ask for. I know he'll be fine, and he'd never in a million years tell me how he's feeling. That's not in his nature at all, but I think he knows I care about him—in fact, we all care about him.

I take a final look around and am ready to go. Beaker has a key and knows where everything is. Simone's nowhere to be found, so I call out goodbye to her, wherever she may be. "Let's see, I have my coat, my gloves, and purse. I'm ready," I say to no one. I pick up the suitcase and open the front door, realizing that when I come back, my circumstances could be quite different. The least that could happen would be for me to be disbarred—the worst, well...I won't even allow myself to go there.

Beaker's already in the office when I arrive and so is my first appointment, a young man who's going to possibly be testifying on behalf of my client who's charged with embezzlement, if this case should even go to trial. He looks terrified, so I get him a coffee and try to ease his fears, telling him that we're just going to talk and that he has nothing to be nervous about. Well, what else would I tell him? Next up, a conference call with the two attorneys with the DA's office, negotiating a plea bargain so that our client, who is a juvenile, won't be charged as an adult for assault. Before I can come up for air, it's almost noon.

When I came in this morning, I placed Dolores's lunch order with Missy. All I've got to do is pick it up at the counter. God bless Missy. I can't believe I'm actually taking a heart patient a cheeseburger, fries, and pie, but the way I see it, Dolores is going to do what she wants anyway, and why shouldn't she if it makes her happy? Life's too short to compromise or settle for what you don't want. I pick up the order, thank Missy, and head out the door.

Dolores lives in a building that's in one of the most sought-after locations in the city, with its breathtaking views of the park. It's pricey, that's for sure, but it's ultra-safe and has amenities that certainly appeal to seniors. Dolores is on the eighth floor, but you must first check in at a separate guard "shack" before entering the main building, show identification, and be granted entrance. It's a lot. I think it might be easier to get into the courthouse or the county jail.

When I finally arrive, Jane opens the door and looks frazzled. "Come on in, she's back in her room and she's all yours. Would you mind reminding her that she needs to take the medication on her bedside table after she eats? Although, that's an exercise in futility, considering what she's just about to consume in that bag." Her eyes narrow on the greasy bag of contraband I'm holding.

"Hey, I'm just delivery, the decision to eat or not is entirely up to her," I say, taking the defense.

"*Hmph!* Well, I'm taking a break and going for a walk. Is it chilly out?"

"It's not too bad, a light jacket should do."

"I'll be back in about thirty minutes. If I don't get out of here soon, I might have to secure your services." She's not smiling.

"Oh my, well, we don't want that. Enjoy your walk."

I tiptoe in, not wanting to disturb her if she's asleep. Dolores is sitting up but dozing. The TV's on, but there's no volume. I see the remote on the other side of the bed and have a feeling that's Jane's way of letting her sister know who's in charge. I place her lunch on her tray and barely have time to release the bag when Dolores stirs. Her eyes flutter open. "Something smells good."

"I didn't mean to wake you."

"That's all I've been doing for the last umpteen days is sleeping. Would you mind bringing that pillow over here and getting that tray?"

I do as I'm told, plumping the extra pillow behind her and sliding her tray towards her. I'm impressed that she has one of those adjustable tables on wheels like the ones they use in hospitals. I go to her bathroom and wash my hands, refill her plastic water tumbler, replace the straw, and set it on the tray, along with her cheeseburger and fries. I pick up her medicine from her side table and put the dosage in a small plastic cup and add that to her lunch tray. "Jane said you gotta take these after you eat."

She ignores me and reaches for the burger. There's an overstuffed reading chair, upholstered in a butterscotch yellow, positioned next to the bed. It looks comfy, but I opt to sit at the foot of the bed.

"Oh, this is heaven," she says with her mouth full. She takes another bite and chews slowly.

I don't talk. Conversation is sometimes overrated. She picks up a fry, takes a bite, then, almost out of exhaustion, sets it down. I don't think she has much appetite. She's just fighting all of this, and all she really wants is to experience something normal, something that doesn't scream *you're ill, you're old!*

"So, you leave later on today, correct?" she asks.

"Yes, I'll go back to the office for a bit, then off to the airport. If you need me at all, call me, or Beaker. No matter what, if you need me, just call," I repeat. "I don't know exactly how long I'll be gone, just a couple days perhaps. And I promise to check in on you while I'm gone."

"You don't have to do that. Don't worry about me. I've got Stalin here and as much as I hate to admit it, she's taking good care of me. Now if you go and tell her I said so, I'll deny it."

"Your word against mine is hard to prove," I state in a matter-of-fact voice.

"That's exactly right. Bertie." She hesitates. "I asked you to come over because I've got something for you. There's a Manila folder on the top of the dresser over there. Would you get that, please?" She is pointing to the tall chest of drawers. "Before my nephew returned to Detroit, I had him go by my bank and get something out of my safety deposit box. It's something I've had for years, and to be perfectly honest, I'd forgotten it was there, but now that you're facing whatever's coming, and because I don't want it to be found by anyone, should something happen to me, I wanted it out of there. For all I know, you probably have already seen it. Anyway, I thought you could decide what to do with it."

"What on earth is it, Dolores?"

"It's the police report of the death of that young man, along with the toxicology report, and the interviews that were conducted during the investigation, if you want to call it that. It's all there."

I'm stunned, unable to speak or move.

She continues. "I had someone years ago obtain the report. Don't worry, this person is exceptionally good at their job, and owed me a favor. Anyway, it makes for some interesting reading. But here's what I think, Bertie. Based on what's in that folder, I'm quite confident that you're going to be just fine."

I'm desperately trying to register what she's saying. Finally, I find my tongue. "I've never seen it. I've been tempted to so many times, but I just couldn't bring myself to look at it. I didn't want to be reminded, and I didn't want to take a chance of rekindling interest in the case. Dolores, I'm scared. What should I do? I'm scared to death to get on that plane. For all I know, I'm walking into a trap. Maybe there'll be authorities there as soon as I come off the plane." I feel like a child, confessing all this fear and vulnerability.

"I'd say you watch too much television. Think about it, if you were going to be arrested, why wouldn't they just take you now and save themselves the trouble of having to bring you back? No, that's hysteria talking. You get on that plane, Bertie. You'll never have any peace until you face it. Let me ask you this. Knowing what you know now, would you have done anything differently?"

"No," I say without a moment's hesitation. I had never asked myself the question Dolores just posed to me.

"Let me tell you something, Bertie. I've spent my entire career watching the injustices of simply being born a woman—having to fight harder, be braver than any man. I've watched women subjected to unbelievable abuse return to their tormentors time and time again, only to wind up dead because of a system that wouldn't protect them. Those abusers, most of the time, walk away as free as a bird. We've come a long way as a society, but we still have a ways to go. I know you, Bertie, so when you tell me you wouldn't have done anything differently, it's because you did what you damn well *had* to do—for yourself, for your friends."

"We were all so young, and so scared. And it happened so fast. But we knew in that instant we'd sealed our fate." I can feel the pain all over again.

1975

TWENTY

Louisville, Kentucky

Audrey's sitting up watching television when we return. She's looks like she's feeling better, still pale but the look on her face tells me she's relieved we're back. None of us wants to be left alone for very long.

"Well, how'd it go?" she asks. "What's the matter? What happened?"

"Eddy's dead." It's all I can get out.

She doesn't react at first. Then she calmly says, "Well, let's face it, down deep inside we already knew that. It was either him or Marie, and *he's* the one who made that choice, not us. He was going to fucking drown her and then quite possibly kill one of us. I refuse to feel any guilt over him and none of you should either." Her voice expresses a cool anger that only Audrey can pull off. "Marie, Eve, we didn't have a choice, did we?" She looks at them for confirmation.

Marie walks over to the chair and collapses. "I owe y'all my life. My only mistake was not dumping him sooner. I was just too weak to stand up to him. I don't know how many times y'all wanted me to walk away. You told me he was going to eventually go too far. I wanted to leave him. I really wanted to, but I couldn't... he—he..." She begins to cry. "He just wouldn't let me go."

"Shhh... It's okay." Eve kneels before her and takes her hands. I rarely see Eve's affectionate side.

I speak up. "This is none of our faults! Eddy brought this on himself. We did it to save Marie, and ourselves, just like Audrey said. We've come this far, and we can't go back now. Eve's parents are wiring her the money tomorrow. Eve, how confident are you that they'll follow through?"

"Oh, you don't have to worry. They'll do it, they will," Eve says as she releases Marie's hands and sits on the edge of the bed. "You can trust them, they're good people. They really are."

"I know, Eve. And I know that phone call must have been hard for you. What you did took courage. We're all in this together," Audrey says, leaning over and touching her shoulder.

"How'd he end up down river, though? It doesn't make sense," Marie says wiping her nose on her t-shirt.

"What do you mean down river?" Audrey says, leaning forward.

"Well, according to what Eve's mom told her over the phone, a man who was fishing early this morning found Eddy's body washed up on the bank of the river, it was about a mile from where we were."

"Are you kidding? How in the hell did he get there?" Audrey asks in disbelief.

"Who knows?" says Marie. "But she said the sheriff's looking for us."

Audrey lets that sink in. It's obvious she's thinking hard. "Bertie, you went back down to get the radio. You didn't hear or see anything." She says it as a statement, not a question. "So, do you think maybe he wasn't dead when we left him, and maybe he, I dunno, tried to get up again, lost his balance, and stumbled into the river?"

I take a few seconds to answer. "It's hard to say. He was drunk and he wasn't moving when we left him. He fell face first and was inches from the water. That's what I remember. We were all so scared—everything's a blur. We were so afraid for Marie; we didn't know if he'd killed her. Once she showed signs of life, we just got the hell out of there!"

"It *don't* matter. I won't change *nothin'*. He's dead and they're looking for us," Marie says with no emotion; there are no more tears.

"So, what's the plan?" Audrey asks.

"Well, for now, we wait on the money. We'll have a better idea of what we'll be able to do then," I say.

On Monday afternoon, we leave Audrey once again for just a little while. We assure her we'll be back soon. I drive Eve and Marie to pick up the money, praying the whole way that it'll be there. Marie and I are relieved when Eve emerges from the building and give us the thumbs up. God bless Mildred and Donald Henderson—they came through for Eve. There's enough there for all of us to have a fighting chance to escape this mess. On our way back, we pass the local movie theater with its marquis displaying movies and showtimes. Marie squeals with excitement as we pass, clapping her hands together and bouncing in her seat like a toddler being given a balloon. "Look, *Jaws* is playing, Bertie! Let's go! C'mon, we've been stuck in that rat hole for days now. Let's have a little fun."

Just hearing her mention that movie makes my gut immediately ache. I think of Billy and my heart is breaking. I swallow hard and try not to cry.

"C'mon, whaddaya say, Bertie? Eve? Let's go!"

Marie's riding up front and is oblivious to my sudden change of mood. She reaches out and gives my shoulder a slight shove. "Let's do it. Pleeease!!!" she squeals again.

I force myself to smile. I'm truly amazed at how Marie can completely ignore the fact that we're running from possible murder charges and she's giddy with the excitement of seeing a horror film. "Okay, listen, I'll circle back, and we'll see what time it's playing tonight, then we'll check on Audrey." I know for a fact that if Marie doesn't do something for fun soon, she's going to be impossible to deal with. It's been hard enough to keep her under control until now. I decide to take a chance. "I'll bring y'all back there to see the movie, and I'll pick you up later. But Marie, you gotta promise me you won't draw any attention to yourself. That means no flirting! If you do, you're going to ruin it for all of us. Do you understand?" I say, no longer trying to hide how serious I am.

"Yeah, I get it. You hear that, Eve? We're going to the movies! Hooray!!"

I hope I haven't made a mistake, but I feel nothing but relief when I pick them up later that evening. Marie literally skips out of the theater with Eve trailing behind. They hop in the car.

"Oh my God, you should have come, it was so cool," Marie says. "I about died every time they played that music, right before that crazy shark was about to attack. *Da-dum, da-dum, da-dum,*" she sings out in a deep throaty voice, mimicking impending doom. "Why, I about peed in my pants, didn't you, Eve?" She throws her head back, cackling. The movie's lifted her spirits and there was no drama except what was on the big screen. I love Marie, I really do, but she's such a loose cannon, and she can be so exhausting.

On Tuesday, we pack our stuff and I check out of the place we've been calling home for four long days. We only stayed this long because of Audrey's situation. We find another place a few miles down the road. It's a little more expensive, but it's an upgrade. By that I mean it's a bit cleaner and doesn't smell as bad. With each day, Audrey seems to be improving. Our room's on the second floor, so we lug our stuff up a flight of stairs. The location's good, and there's plenty of fast food restaurants and gas station mini marts within walking distance. That'll save on gas. I'm a puddle by the time we get settled in the room. I turn the air conditioning on full blast and put my face directly in front of the unit. Once my temperature begins to come back to normal, I say, "Okay, it's time to get serious. We need to come up with some plans and decide where to go from here."

By the look on their faces, I realize I'm going to have to start. I begin to share some of my thoughts. First up, what to do about Audrey's car, since it's registered in Estill County, has Estill County plates, and we don't have the title. We need to get rid of it—they'll be looking for it. All of us agree Marie's the best candidate to accomplish this. She can persuade almost any man to do anything, with very little effort.

Next, Audrey's still not at her best, but she can help by using a phone. She's in charge of calling the Greyhound Bus station and finding out schedules and fares. Eve's job is to do some research in the library, looking up the locations and information regarding two cities of interest, New York and Washington, DC. I give her a list of things that'll be helpful in an unfamiliar town. Audrey and I have decided to remain in Louisville for now, at least until she feels strong and ready to travel. I told her that I wasn't going anywhere with her until she's examined by a doctor. She's not happy with me. I don't care. Yesterday I went to the post office and obtained a P.O. box, at least now we have a place where communication is possible, for a while anyway, until we're all safely off the grid. I think it's important we partially split up. Why? Because I'm trying to think like a man, and I believe they'll think that because we're girls, we'll stick together. I have no idea whether my assumptions are right, but I'm doing the best I can building the airplane as I fly it, hoping it doesn't crash.

By the end of the week, we still haven't heard any news come over the television or seen any articles in the Louisville paper regarding Eddy's death or four missing Estill County girls. Eve doesn't plan on contacting her folks again any time soon, at least not until she's settled somewhere and thinks it's safe. Who knows when that might be? I think we've made some strides, though. Marie's been successful at her task and has managed to sweet-talk balding Earl from Earl's Used Cars into trading in the Comet for a gold '68 Chevy Impala with over 100,000 miles. Marie's a master—that she is. I should never underestimate her. She and Eve have decided they will take a bus to New York City. That's where Eve has always wanted to go, and it's sure as hell the best choice for getting entirely lost. I can't help but think that with Eve's talent, and Marie's—well, Marie's assets, they'll be fine. Audrey has the bus schedule and tells them that it looks like they can leave early Saturday morning. We decide to give ourselves a little party Friday night. We draw names so that we can give each person a small gift, nothing expensive, just a little something to remember each other by. We get laughing hysterically when it takes us three tries to draw someone else's name other than our own. We make a quick trip to the local Ayr-Way, leaving Audrey once again in the room to stay put and rest, but I've been given strict instructions on what to get for the person whose name she has drawn. After quickly shopping, we stop at the bakery, taking the only cake left in the display case, a yellow cake with vanilla icing and red roses that reads "Happy Birthday Fred." It was never picked up. We don't care.

We carry everything back to the room, and Eve places the cake on a small table that's in front of the window. We hurry and exchange our gifts, afraid the ice cream will melt if we're not quick. Eve hands Audrey her gift. Audrey opens the tiny box and lifts out a small silver heart necklace.

"It's beautiful, Eve. Thank you!" Audrey says as she hugs her.

"It might turn your neck green, but you'll have an extra heart for a while," Eve says.

Audrey hands her gift to Marie. Marie opens the bag. It's a sparkly pink plastic makeup bag filled with little lipsticks, blushes, and eyeshadows. There's even a small glamour brush inside.

"Well, you couldn't have had Bertie get anything prettier. I just love it," Marie says hugging Audrey.

Marie then hands me my gift. It's a small bottle of perfume. I open it and spray a little on my wrist. It smells of roses and, well, something rather earthy. "My first perfume. Thank you, Marie," I say, spraying a little sample on everyone's wrist.

"Well, it's sophisticated. Perfume's a grown-up thing, and you've been the grown-up, Bertie."

I choke up but shake it off and hand Eve her present. She opens it and her eyes shine. It's a blue bound diary and an assortment of colored pens. "You gotta keep writing, Eve, okay?"

"I promise, I will," she says as she clutches the diary and pens to her chest.

"Okay, that's enough! Let's eat cake before we all end up in tears," I say. To our surprise, Eve pulls out a lighter and a pack of candles she bought at the store.

"I know it's not anyone's birthday, but I thought we could all use a little something special before we say goodbye," Eve says. She places four candles in the cake and lights them. Marie's standing next to me and she reaches out and takes my hand. I do the same with Audrey's, and Audrey takes Eve's.

"Wait, wait, let's make a pledge," Marie says emphatically. "Let's agree that we'll keep our secret, and no matter where we go, if any of us are ever in trouble, we'll be there for each other." She says this in a more serious tone than I've ever heard coming from Marie.

"How will we do that?" Audrey asks.

"Well..." Marie thinks a moment before she continues. "We'll have a word that we'll use if any of us need help. All we'll have to do is use the word if we're ever in trouble and afraid to use our names. We might be able to call or write, or whatever, and we'll do everything in our power to help each other," Marie says. "We have the post office box now, so for now we can get word to each other, right?" She looks around at each of us.

"Yeah, sure, let's do it," I say.

"I'm in," says Audrey.

"Me too," adds Eve.

"So, what's our word?" I ask looking for a suggestion.

"Fireflies," Eve says with a smile.

We all grin, nod, and blow out the candles.

Present Day

TWENTY-ONE

I leave Dolores in good hands and return to the office before heading to the airport. Beaker's on the phone and Annie's door is shut, so I check my messages and emails. I find only work-related things, and items that I can defer until next week. Nothing else has come through that would change the plans. My stomach's in a knot, but I do my best to push through it, telling myself I'm fine. I send a quick email, shut down my computer, grab my coat and purse, and head out. I stop at Annie's door but don't hear any one-sided conversation, so I tap lightly.

"Come in," she says.

Poking my head in, I say, "Hey, I'm heading to the airport. I'll call you as soon as I land."

"Okay." She stops for a minute and gives me a hard look. "You're nervous, aren't you?"

She knows me too well. "I'd be lying if I said I'm not…. When I get back, I promise we'll talk."

Annie comes around the desk and gives me a hug. I hold her a bit longer this time, kissing her on the side of her head like I did when she was little. Her hair smells of citrus.

"You take care of yourself and that grandbaby of mine, okay?"

"I promise."

"Love you," I say.

"Love you too! Save travels. Don't forget to call me!" She hurries to sit back at her desk. "And Mom, I don't know what's happening, but I hope it turns out well. I really do."

"Me too." If I look at her much longer, I might not board the plane, so I wave goodbye and leave.

Beaker's talking through his earpiece, so I mouth a thank you and pantomime that I'll call him. He gives me a thumbs up.

By three o'clock, I'm sitting in the airport watching a young mother corral a toddler who keeps escaping her grasp, and the young bearded fellow wearing headphones seated next to me is intensely concentrating on his laptop. He reminds me of Beaker. There's an elderly couple sitting across the way. She keeps fussing at her husband to check his carry-on for his medication. *These are the symptoms of everyday life. Aren't they a beautiful thing?*

I board the plane and stow my suitcase in the compartment above my seat. Luckily, I was able to get a window seat, so I slide in, fortunate not to crack my head in the process. A young man wearing a University of Kentucky jersey takes the seat next to me. For a moment, I feel a twinge of apprehension, remembering another young man who was planning on attending that same university on a football scholarship. A woman a few years younger than me with huge hoop earrings and a colorful bright orange scarf takes the aisle seat. It's not long before we're in the air.

I gaze out the window as we float above the clouds. I wonder if this is what heaven really looks like, and if it is, then I pray Joe's up there somewhere watching over me. I miss him so much. I miss his laugh, his smile, his voice, but most of all, I miss his touch. I know what he'd tell me if he were here. He'd say, *"Bertie, you got this."*

I hope you're right, Joe.

I shift in my seat and stretch my legs. There's never enough room in these seats and my foot kicks my purse that I've shoved under the seat in front of me. I can see the Manila folder peeking out from my handbag. I've been agonizing over when to read it since Dolores presented it to me this afternoon. I was tempted to sit and read it in the car as soon as I left Dolores's, but I couldn't bring myself to. I thought about closing my door to my office and looking at it then, but I didn't want to with Annie and Beaker around and possible interruptions. Now it's just sitting there, begging me to read it, but because of its most likely contents, not to mention my proximity to the other passengers, probably not a good place to do any crime scene reading. Besides, if I'm being honest, I'm afraid I might just come unglued when I do look at it, and I in no way need to be doing that around anyone. I've already decided I'll wait until I'm in the hotel room to look at it.

I'm deep in thought when the pilot announces that we'll be landing shortly. I will myself to stay calm. The landing is smooth, and it's not long before I'm rolling my carry-on behind me and up the ramp to enter Ronald Reagan National Airport. I move quickly but am watchful and secretly pray there's no one there to greet me sporting a police badge. Paranoia has its function, and I'm utilizing it right now.

I follow the signs to the Hertz Car Rental and within the hour, I am driving off the lot with a 2019 black Range Rover and on my way to the hotel. My body's literally running on fumes when I finally enter the lobby of the hotel. Any other time, I might be impressed with the hotel's contemporary design and its sleek modern look, not to mention the luxurious amenities they offer. But it's wasted on me. I've come a long way from the trashy motels the girls and I experienced so long ago, but in the end, none of it matters because I'm not enjoying this five-star wonder any more than I did the smelly one-star flea-infested motel. All I want to do right now is check in and hide.

My room is located on the tenth floor and is everything you would expect from an upscale hotel, spacious with a queen-sized bed clothed in gold and white bedding, not a wrinkle to be found, not a corner that isn't tucked military tight. Plush matching gold-tufted throw pillows adorn the bedspread that serve no other purpose than adding to the cost of the room. It's all pristine and meticulous until I throw my suitcase, purse, and coat on the bed. I don't open the curtains because I don't give a damn about the view. I head straight for the shower and try to wash away the last twelve hours. I towel dry my hair and put on a pair of pale pink cotton pajamas and my lightweight wraparound robe. I haven't eaten anything since this morning, so I order a club sandwich from room service and then check out the minibar, selecting a small bottle of chardonnay and a pack of peanut M&M's. What can I say? I don't have expensive taste.

My sandwich arrives and I grab one of the complimentary bottles of Evian off the dresser and take my sandwich to the bed. I don't turn on the television. I just sit and eat, occasionally sipping water from the bottle. The sandwich is delicious, and I chew slowly, savoring the moment as I think about Dolores and her cheeseburger. About halfway through my meal I've had enough and set everything aside. The folder is sitting on the other side of the bed, waiting patiently for me to give it some attention. I reach over and pick it up, but before I open it, I take the Chardonnay, unscrew the top, and take two healthy swigs. I take a breath and open the folder.

The first document is a police report filed with the Irvine sheriff's department by Robert Dennison, father of Edward D. Dennison, reporting his son missing on the morning of Sunday, July 13, 1975. According to the report, the last time anyone in the family saw Eddy was sometime early Friday afternoon. Neither his mother nor his father got worried until he failed to return home Saturday evening. They said it wasn't all that unusual for their son to stay over with friends, especially on the weekends. When Sunday morning came and he still wasn't home, Mr. Dennison tried calling Eddy's friends, but no one had seen him. Mr. Dennison also made a call to his son's girlfriend, Marie Parker, but was told by Marie's parents that she hadn't returned home either. That's when he decided to go to the police.

The next document describes what happened almost immediately following Mr. Dennison's reporting his son missing. A local by the name of Charles Proctor was fishing early Sunday morning when he saw what looked to be a body floating near the banks of the Kentucky River. He immediately made a call to the Irvine sheriff's department. The time was 8:52 a.m., exactly ten minutes after Robert Dennison reported his son missing. The sheriff's department found the body of a young male along the banks of the Kentucky River, two miles northwest of the town of Irvine. Sheriff Virgil Fairfield and Deputy Joseph Bailey arrived at the scene. By the time they arrived, word had already gotten out and several interested onlookers were congregating along the banks. Two boys stood within three feet of the body when authorities arrived—John Kellogg, age 14, and Bobby Martin, age 12. The sheriff and deputy proceeded to tape off the perimeter and secure the scene. Eddy's car, a 1970 Red Plymouth Barracuda, was located on one of the back roads less than a quarter mile from where the body was found. The keys were still in the ignition.

I take all this in. So, he was found more than a mile from where we left him on the bank of the river. The fact that several people arrived at the site, compromising the integrity of the crime scene, is both the police and prosecutor's nightmare. However, that wasn't the actual crime scene. So far, I haven't seen anything indicating they ever identified the real crime scene, at least not yet. The fact that I'm even using the term "crime scene" makes me uncomfortable. The real crime was Eddy's assault on Marie. I turn my attention to Eddy's car—that's a whole other matter. It should have been located somewhere closer to where we were, not that far down the river. I often wondered where Eddy parked his car that night and how long he'd been waiting to see if we'd show up. Questions I may never have answers to, but I have a theory. I keep going. I've got more ground to cover and the next item in the folder is the one I've dreaded the most. There's a smaller envelope still left unopened. I can almost guarantee what's in it—crime scene photos. So, I reach over and take another chug of wine; it burns my throat going down. I chase it with the water, and then pull the photos out. I'm immediately confronted with horror in black and white, Eddy's bloating body, half floating in the water, the other half tangled in weeds on the muddy bank of the Kentucky River. I'm immediately sick and the contents of what I've eaten erupts. I run to the bathroom just in time to reach the toilet. The smell of wine and vomit fill my nose and mouth, only causing me to wretch in violent waves. When there's nothing more to give, I grip the sides of the toilet and wait until I can feel my legs again and I'm able to rise without falling flat on my face. I knew it was going to be bad but seeing those photos has a far greater effect on me than I could ever have imagined. There's a white washcloth folded in the shape of small bird on the bathroom counter, and I show it no respect, plunging it under cold water, wringing it out, and wiping my face and mouth. I remove the paper top of the drinking glass sitting next to the sink and rinse my mouth, then brush my teeth and rinse again.

When I emerge from the bathroom, one photo is lying on the floor, the other two still on the bed. They're all taken from slightly different angles. I've seen hundreds of photos in my career as a defense attorney—horrible, tragic stuff—but until this moment I did not understand the trauma my clients must have endured when presented with the scenes of the crimes they were on trial for.

Averting my eyes the best I can, I gather up the photos, place them back into the envelope and force myself to continue. The next item is the autopsy and toxology report. His blood alcohol was 0.21. I knew it had to have been at a high level because of his out-of-control behavior. I can still see him staggering, stopping short of our little campsite, reaching into his back pocket, and pulling out the bottle. He was weaving when he chugged the rest, then launched the bottle into the brush.

The autopsy reveals several contusions to his upper back and shoulders, scratches and nail marks around his neck, arms, and hands. I remember desperately scratching and clawing at him, trying to get him to let Marie up for air. He just wouldn't stop. It further describes a contusion to the lower right side of the skull (occipital bone) causing inflammation and swelling, most likely from blunt force. Water was found to be present in the lungs. They estimate the time of death to be sometime between late Friday evening of the 11th or the early morning hours of Saturday, the 12th. Cause of death: Drowning, classified as a homicide.

I lie back. It's almost too much reliving that night. He died of drowning, not Eve's blow to the head with her massive flashlight. There's a clearer picture forming. I wasn't thinking straight that night, and I was operating on terror and adrenaline, not to mention we had all done a bit of partying. I never told any of the girls what I saw when I returned for the radio and my own conclusions, but I really couldn't be sure. I just needed to get the hell out of there, leaving as little evidence as possible that we were ever there. And, oh God, Eve! Eve felt such guilt over what she thought she had done, yet Marie and the rest of us continued to assure her that she saved Marie's life that night, and though the rest of us tried to stop him, only Eve's final blow ended Eddy's reign of terror and allowed us to get away. As far as the flashlights, well, they were tossed long ago. I wonder if Eve ever found out she wasn't responsible for his death, or if somehow Eve's parents were aware of the results of the autopsy. Word travels fast in a small town. I know she sometimes stayed in contact with her parents because she would occasionally forward information to me through the post office box—that's how I found out about Mama's passing. All correspondence with the girls stopped several years ago, and I eventually closed the post office box. So many years have gone by, and, well, if I'm being truly honest, I was hoping that all this, and yes, even my old friends, would stay in the past. I feel ashamed of so many things, but mostly of being an imposter, hiding in plain sight my entire life. And then there's the hypocrisy—me, standing up in front of jurors, talking about the importance of truth. But the worst part is looking at my daughter's face and knowing I've never been able to tell her the truth about her grandmother, about my best friends, or about Estill County. I wonder what she'll think of me when I tell her, and I *will* tell her, because I've run the clock down. No matter what, it's time.

I get up and pace the room, go into the bathroom, and let cold water run through my fingers, once again letting it be my calming agent as I splash my face and neck. I'm determined to get through the entire contents before I meet with whomever, and face whatever's in store for me tomorrow. I massage my stiff neck with both hands and return to the bed, picking up the last few pages and vowing that I will face this and read every single word.

I read the initial interviews with Eddy's family members, his parents, and his younger sister. Eddy's mother and sister stated that the last time they remember seeing Eddy was sometime Friday in the early afternoon, and his father said he hadn't actually seen him since the night before, because he left for work early Friday morning before his son got up. The entire family does point to Marie as being someone the police should speak with. None of them could recall Eddy having any enemies; he was so loved by everyone in the community. I think several in town might have disputed that.

The remaining pages of the report consist of interviews conducted with the other members of the town that saw him in the last forty-eight-hour period before his death. My attention is suddenly drawn to the interview conducted on Monday, July 14, with none other than Glennis Campbell. I brace myself.

It begins with Deputy Bailey asking Glennis Campbell the last time she saw her daughter or her daughter's friends and whether her daughter ever told her about having any problems with Eddy Dennison. Mama started by saying that you'd have to be deaf, dumb, and blind in this town if you hadn't had any trouble with Eddy Dennison. I can literally hear Mama's voice in my head as she delivers her editorial comments. But, no, she doesn't remember her daughter having any specific problems with him. As far as where her daughter and friends were, well, they were all at her house Friday night. Yes, all of them. She swears Marie, Audrey, and Eve were all there. They came in shortly after Glennis came home from work, maybe about 5:30 p.m. or so. She said she was surprised when they showed up because she thought they had plans to go out but decided at the last minute it was just too hot, so they stayed at the house, listening to records, doing each other's hair—you know, stuff girls do. She went on to tell the deputy that come morning, they were all up early and that Bertie told her that she and her friends had decided they wanted to go live their dreams. They left somewhere after nine a.m. and that's the last she's seen or heard from her daughter.

I reread her interview over and over again. Mama had flat-out lied. Her sworn statement gave us all an alibi, and whether they believed her or not—which I doubt seriously they did—it's enough to shed doubt on our involvement. I'm stunned. I'm really, really stunned.

I look through what's left of the interviews, and I don't see any mention of us being seen at the bar in

Richmond, nor anything else that could implicate us. I go back to Mama's interview and still can't believe it. She's no longer around to testify, having died of cirrhosis of the liver five years after I left. She covered for us. Glennis Campbell had finally, for once in her life, done what any mother would have done. She protected her child and at the same time protected Marie, Audrey, and Eve. I can hardly believe we most likely owe our future to Glennis Campbell.

Present Day

TWENTY-TWO

Crime scene photos are haunting me in this dark hotel room and the ghastly whispers of autopsy results and interviews play in my head, keeping me awake. I'm physically and emotionally numb, and it's not over. It may never be. I look at the clock. It's 4:37 a.m. I turn over and shut my eyes tight but may brain has no off switch. What's in store today? Is it Audrey, or Marie, or Eve reaching out to warn me of something? Or maybe one or more of them need help themselves. Could it be blackmail, a trap, or maybe even an arrest? Am I a fool for coming? But we promised each other that if we were in trouble, we would use the word *fireflies*, and we'd come. I smile sadly in the dark at the naiveté of our youth; we couldn't see past the next day, let alone years that turned into a lifetime. We were so young and petrified to face an uncertain world on the run. I'm taking a gamble that I was summoned for good reason, and it will be in my best interest to have come. I'm betting against the house, as Dolores would say. I've been reacting emotionally, and I know better as an attorney. I think about the file I spent last night forcing myself to examine, and it gives me a little hope. The part of the river where Eddy's body was found was compromised and there is absolutely no mention of any other place along the river that might have been considered a crime scene. The body had been in the water for over twenty-four hours, and there was no physical evidence. DNA evidence wasn't around at the time, and the river would have most likely washed away any traces anyway. And then there's Mama's interview, the most shocking thing I found in the entire file, the complete fabrication of our whereabouts. Adding all that up, I don't think there's a district attorney anywhere who would want to touch this. There's enough reasonable doubt not to warrant the conviction of any of us, but Lady Justice can be tricky. *Oh God!* This is making me crazy, so I throw off the covers, surrendering my slumber like a white flag claiming defeat. It's futile, so I get up and look at the clock. It's 6:15 a.m. I shove my feet into my slippers and do what I didn't do last night when I arrived—open the drapes and peek at the outside world. I watch the sun begin to rise as it plays hide-and-go-seek between the space of two buildings along the skyline. I order a pot of coffee and some toast from room service and turn on the television. I still have a few hours, and, strangely enough, I'm not totally jumping out of my skin. My coffee arrives and it smells divine, a deep dark French roast, so I take my time and savor each sip as if it were my last. I butter a piece of toast and add some orange marmalade from the fancy sealed jars. I don't have much appetite, but I force myself to get something into my stomach. I took a shower last night, but I decide to take another. I need the jolt that only a shower can give. I step out, towel-dry my hair, and throw open my suitcase. I dress in khakis and a black cardigan over a white oxford shirt, and I slip on a pair of sensible walking shoes. My hair is still damp, so I quickly blow-dry it and leave it loose around my shoulders. Once again, I think I'm probably too old to continue wearing it this long but it's the one thing I still hang onto. I even hear Mama's voice telling me not to cut my hair. I would think that her advice would've been reason enough for me to have chopped it off years ago. Silver streaks, not gray, but true silver pop up here and there, and that's okay. I apply a little foundation to my face, dab on coral lip gloss for a little shine, add some blush and a touch of mascara. I stare at myself in the mirror and try to picture myself at eighteen. I've spent my whole life trying to wipe that girl away. I should have known that I could never totally erase her. She's my shadow.

I grab my laptop and decide to look again at where I'm going. I bring up the address and find an image of the neighborhood. It seems like a lovely place in Arlington that might have been developed sometime in the 1980s based on the architecture of the houses along the block. Seems to be home to upper-middle class families who settled there to raise their children. I've often thought of Audrey, wondering whether she had children. I know how difficult it was during the miscarriage and the horrible circumstances surrounding the unwanted pregnancy and then the loss. I wonder if she ever forgave her father. What he did far exceeded the pain Mama inflicted on me, but we shared deep emotional scars regardless. The bizarre thing is that she probably deep down still loves her father. I want to love Mama, I really do, but I'm void of feelings. I can't even say I hate her anymore.

I glance at my watch and come to terms with the fact that it's time. The valet takes all of ten minutes to bring the car around and in another two minutes, I leave the hotel and follow my GPS, heading for Audrey's. It's a fabulous day, and I'll just bet it'll be hopping with visitors to our nation's capital. This is perfect weather for sightseeing. I find a radio station that's playing soft rock, reach over and grab my sunglasses out of my purse and put them on, shielding my eyes from these brilliant sunny skies. A totally cloud-free morning. My senses must be on high alert. I even notice the abundance of blooming daffodils etching the walkways, resembling tiny yellow spectators lining the streets for a spring parade. Tourists with their cameras and smartphones walk with gaggles of children of all sizes along the sidewalks, poised and ready to take that perfect photograph. I envy these people out exploring, who will maybe later make their way across the Potomac to see the Lincoln Memorial or one of the museums by way of the National Mall. What I wouldn't give to be one of them taking in the sights and enjoying the day.

There's traffic and construction that I don't anticipate in my drive time, so I try to remain calm and not lose my nerve as I wait and wait and wait. What if I'm late? Is it a good thing or a bad thing? I break through the congestion and move along. Not quickly, but I'm moving. Eventually I find myself nearby and make a left turn into the entrance to the neighborhood, fifteen minutes shy of on time. I locate the street and immediately recognize the surroundings from the Google street views. It's a comforting neighborhood—families and dogs. Even with my windows up, I can hear the shrieks of children playing. There's a couple of kiddos on Big Wheels racing up and down their driveway, their mothers chatting on the sidewalk while keeping a watchful eye on the little racers. An elderly woman in a lavender tracksuit and tennis shoes is walking a Pomeranian. The neighborhood is full of trees, and most of the houses have sprawling front yards. I slow down until I see the house number and then come to a stop at the driveway, surveying the scene before pulling in. The house is a large rambling ranch with red brick and white trim. There's a huge picture window in front that looks out onto a well-manicured lawn. Two cars are in the driveway, all with Virginia license plates, so I wonder if they belong to Virginia residents, or maybe they're rentals like my own. Only one way to find out. I park behind a black Honda CRV and cautiously get out of the car and make my way to the front door. I take a deep breath and ring the doorbell. I think I hear women laughing but can't be sure. I lean in trying to listen more intently when the front door opens and a handsome guy with a full beard and mustache appears.

"I—I'm here to....to...I'm......" I'm unable to form a cohesive thought, let alone formulate a sentence.

A huge smile flashes across his face. "I think I know who you are! You must be Bertie. I'm Mike, Audrey's husband. Please, please come in," he says, grabbing my hand and pulling me into the foyer. "She is going to be so happy to see you." He exudes genuine warmth and enthusiasm, still holding onto my hand tightly. Another burst of laughter erupts and now I know beyond a doubt it's women's voices I hear.

"So, it was Audrey that sent for me?" I ask with both relief and the need for reassurance.

"Oh yeah, she did. She sent for all of you. She wasn't sure you'd come, but I told her you'd come. I know this must be difficult for all of you. But let me assure you, there's no need to be worried. Over the years, Audrey's shared everything with me. I know the story and I promise you, you're safe. You are all safe here," Mike says.

"Really? All of us, we're all here?" I begin to shake. I don't know why, but I can't control it.

As if we've known each other for years, Mike takes both of my hands. His hands are warm and sturdy. "Bertie," he looks directly into my eyes, "she has asked you and the others here for a reason. It's important that you understand the situation before you go in to see her." He stops and looks up at the ceiling, then starts again. "Audrey has metastatic breast cancer, and she's refusing any further treatment. She wants you here, she brought you here..." He stammers, then clears his throat. "She brought you here," he begins again, his inflection deep and intentional, "to say goodbye."

"Goodbye?" The words finally hit home. "Oh my God, no, no. This is just, it's...this is so unfair. Oh God, Audrey."

"Believe it or not, she's really at peace with her decision. She's been dealing with this for many years, but she wants to see you, Bertie. She's in the den with Marie and Eve. She does well this time of the day, and she wanted to be at her best when she saw all of you. She had a rough week following her first email to you, so that's why there was a delay in reaching out to you again. But she's rallied a bit and strong enough for now. She's ready and so anxious to see you. Are you ready?"

I shake my head yes. I do want to see her. My heart is hurting, and he gently releases my hands, and I follow him in slow motion down the hall. It all seems so surreal. I step across the threshold, as if reaching the other side of a time portal. I come face to face with the women who share my secret. Marie is first to jump up, throwing her arms around me in a massive bear hug. "Oh, my God! Bertie, it's so good to see you!" She's still a beauty, platinum shoulder-length hair, gone are her curls. Her thick lashes and beautiful complexion take ten years off her age, not to mention her voluptuous curves in all the right places, as evident by her form-fitting animal-print dress and sheer black hose. She completes her look with bangled, gold bracelets and a pair of low-slung heels the color of caramel. I hug her back, clinging to her like a life raft until she finally releases me.

Eve rises—no, floats across the room—taking my hands in hers. "Hello, dear friend. It's wonderful to see you," she says, her words like silk. Eve looks every bit the native New Yorker she's become, still petite and slender, hair that's almost ink black in a severe, chin-length bob with bangs. She's wearing a black turtleneck over black slacks and black ankle boots, an outfit reserved for much cooler temperatures, but just the thing Eve would wear. A silver medallion of some modern artistic design hangs from a long, braided chain around her neck. The overall look resembles that of a female villain in an animated motion picture. It's her round doe eyes that have remained the same. No amount of New York chic has been able to completely erase the young, innocent girl I still see in shadows of her eyes.

I turn my attention to Audrey. There's no mistaking it's my friend curled on the end of the sofa, her auburn locks now replaced with a peacock blue scarf, her oval face thin but strangely radiant. She's aged and her skin looks opaque, yet still so very lovely. I step forward, at least I try to move, but I find myself almost paralyzed with emotion. I can barely find my voice as I croak out, "Aud... Audrey. Oh, Audrey."

"Hello, Bertie," Audrey says as she lifts her arms to me. Her face registers calmness, serenity.

Tears roll down my face. I wipe them away, crossing the room and wrapping my arms around her thin frame, burying my head in the sharp blade of her collar bone. "Oh, Audrey, I'm so very sorry." I cry. She cradles me as I sob in her arms. Pent-up emotions are released, and I can't help but let them escape. I feel arms around me. Marie and Eve are with us. We are together again.

"Shh, it's alright, Bertie. Everything's alright," Audrey says as she gently holds me in her arms. "Don't be sad, Bertie, we had a hell of a run, didn't we? Didn't we all?" she says to all of us.

"We sure as hell have," says Marie.

"We made it, didn't we? And we did it with each other's help," Eve says.

Lifting my face, I look at all of them. "Oh my God, it's so good to see all of you. I can't tell you how often I've thought about you." I wipe my face with my sleeve. Audrey reaches out and grabs a tissue from the box off the side table and hands it to me. I accept it, marveling at her ability to give comfort to me when it's me who should be comforting her.

"Audrey, I wish I would have known sooner. I would have come. I swear," I say.

"We all would have come," Marie chimes in.

"In a New York minute," Eve says with a smile.

"Well, you're here now, and that's what's important. I certainly didn't want to put any of you at risk, but I wanted to see you all again and thank you and tell you I love you all. I apologize for the email, but I didn't want to expose any of you unnecessarily. I struggled with whether I should even reach out or not."

"Oh, Audrey, I'm so glad you did, I'm so glad we're together." I'm genuinely overwhelmed with emotion.

Marie agrees. "Me too. I admit that at first, I didn't know what to do. It scared the bejeezus outta me, so I broke my own rule and reached out to you and Eve," she says looking at me. "I wanted to know if you all had gotten the message and were coming. I reached Eve. But, Bertie, I'm sorry, it was me who left that message about the box at your office. I kind of panicked."

"Oh hell, Marie, that scared the shit out of me," I laugh as I wipe my tears and blow my nose. "But it doesn't matter. We made a promise that we'd be here for each other when needed, and that's what we've done." I focus on Audrey. "You're remarkable dealing with this. How long have you known, um, I mean, how have you been getting through...?" I don't know how to finish. I remain at Audrey's side while Marie and Eve pull up an ottoman to share and sit close.

Audrey gives a sad sigh and holds onto my hands. "Oh, for quite a while. The apple hasn't fallen too far from the tree, right? My ma was only forty-one when this unforgiving disease took her, and I swore I'd fight it, but I soon discovered it's not a war to be won. For me it's been a set of continuous hoops to jump through. It's been twelve years since I was first diagnosed with breast cancer. How have I dealt with it?" She thought for a moment. "It's been endless doctor visits to find out when my lease on life might be up, or if just maybe I've bought a little more time with the next round of treatments. It's weeks of radiation, chemotherapy, hormone therapy, and all the other kinds of therapy they've thrown on the wall to see what might stick. Then there's the surgeries, blood tests, and scans. It's doing the worst kind of homework that involves studying my own lab results, hoping and praying for some positive numbers, but instead finding out that despite all the efforts, it's now gone to the lungs, the liver, and the stomach. It's looking into the faces of friends who want to help, but don't know how and don't know what to say. It's trying to live as normal a life as I can because that's all I can do. It's holding my husband's hand knowing that he will be left alone to deal with the aftermath. But even with all of it, and as hard as all this has been, the day I was told that children would never be in my future, that day was far worse. So, that's the unpretty truth. But I'm still here, and today I have my friends with me, and the love of my life is in the next room."

"Like I said, you're really remarkable." I am squeezing her hands.

"I'm not remarkable, just been living with this illness and doing what any of you would do in the same situation. No, I'm not remarkable, but I've got remarkable friends and an incredibly supportive husband." She has conviction in her eyes.

"Well, I'd say we're all pretty badass if you ask me," Marie says with a grin and cutting through the macabre conversation.

"Yes, we are, Marie. We certainly are. I wanted to see all of you again. I wanted to tell each one of you that because of you, I've been able to live my life on my terms. I can't imagine what my life would've been like otherwise. Don't get me wrong, everything about this illness sucks, but I've had these coveted years since we all left Estill County, and I wouldn't have traded them for anything. Mike's been my rock and confidant, he knows everything, and I don't know what I would have done without him."

Eve surprises us by speaking up. "I know how it feels to have someone to confide in. My partner Jackie knows everything, and I eventually told Mom, too. Jackie and I've been together for well over thirty years. I don't know what would have happened to me if I'd stayed in Estill County. New York gave me my love, my dream, my ability to write, but most importantly, my freedom. I was no longer the eccentric freak, because everyone I know now pretty much fits that category. For the first time in my life, I found a place to belong. I never would've had the courage to leave if it wasn't for all of you."

Marie's tone takes on a sad note. "I've never spoken of that night to anyone. Can y'all believe that? Three husbands, and I haven't breathed a single, solitary word to any of them, but I do think about what happened that night from time to time. Don't get me wrong, I feel zero guilt, and I've certainly never let it consume me. Eddy got what was comin' to him. If he hadn't been such an asshole, he could've been really *somethin'*, he could've been a pro-football player, maybe famous or somethin'. I never could understand what made that boy so mean. I think it was his daddy, 'cause he was awful rough on him. But I don't for one single solitary minute feel any guilt. Hell, he damn-near killed me that night. And Eve—well, all of you saved me."

"Yeah, but none of us killed him." By the expression on their faces, I have their attention. I swallow hard because it's painful just thinking about that horrible night, let alone speaking about it out loud. It makes it all the more real, raw. I force myself continue. "I'm serious. We didn't kill him. He didn't die from a blow to the head from Eve's flashlight. He drowned." I give them a moment to let that sink in before pressing on. "I read the autopsy and police reports last night for the first time. Believe me when I say I never wanted to, never! I was too scared and didn't want to face it. I also didn't want to take a chance on raising suspicion. I never intentionally sought it out. Someone I trust secretly acquired a copy of the reports and gave them to me. I spent all of last night reading them—well, that and vomiting," I admit with a weak smile. "It was really hard, but I'm so glad I did. Do you all want to hear the details?" I ask before venturing down that path. They collectively shake their heads yes. I spend the next tortuous minutes describing in vivid detail what was in the reports. By the time I finish, the room is so quiet, all I can hear is the sound of Mike moving around in the next room.

"My God, you mean he really did drown?" Marie asks, stunned. "We never really knew for sure."

"Yes, remember Eve's parents said as much but we thought it might've just been rumors. I, uh, we really didn't know for sure." I falter in my response but catch myself.

"And your mama told them we were all together at your house all night?" Marie repeats floored by the news. "*Your* mama? Glennis Campbell? Well, I'll be damned."

"Hard to believe, isn't it?" I look over at Eve and she looks to be in a daze. "Eve, you okay?"

"I didn't kill him…" she says, her stunned expression trying hard to process the news.

"No, Eve, you didn't kill him," I answer.

"You suppose he gained consciousness and staggered into the water himself?" Audrey finally asks.

I think cautiously before answering her question, the same question she asked decades ago, because what I really saw when returning to the river to retrieve Eve's radio is the part I've never shared with anyone and won't now either. "I don't think we'll ever know for sure what happened, but I'm not afraid anymore and neither should any of you be. We're not responsible for Eddy's death, and from what I've seen in the report, it's just not a case they can prove against us, especially a cold case like this one."

"I've wasted too many years with those ghosts," Marie remarks.

"Eve, I've always wanted to thank you for sending word about my mother," I say sincerely.

"My parents are both gone," Eve says somberly. "I even managed to bring my mother to New York after my father died, but she only lasted another year. It was good having her close though. You know what she said to me before she died? She said that all she really wanted was for me to be happy."

"I haven't laid eyes on my parents since I left," Marie says. "I heard they died years ago. I've had my ways of finding out bits and pieces of information over the years. I've had some fairly rich husbands with connections, if you know what I mean," Marie says with a wink.

A shadow of sadness changes her face. "I'd be surprised if my folks ever cared one minute that I was gone. After my brother died, they didn't seem to care about much of anything. Do you know they didn't even report me missing? What does that tell ya?" She's shaking her perfectly coiffed head.

"I never even changed my name until I married Joe," I confess. "I figured it was to my advantage to hide in plain sight, so that's what I did. Nobody ever came looking for us. I never left Louisville, I was planning on staying after Audrey left, just for a little while longer to make sure we were all safe and that we could reach each other through the post office box. But I guess I stayed too long because I fell in love with Louisville. I spent those first few years bartending and waitressing at night, trying to make enough money to go to school. Eventually I even made it through law school, becoming an attorney. I think deep down I'm still and always will be the defiant one. I guess it's in my nature—maybe that's why I went into criminal law. Looking back, I think in those early years I was just plain pissed at the world and dared the law to come find me. If there was one thing Glennis Campbell taught me, it was to always be ready for a fight and know how to win."

"I remember saying goodbye to you, Bertie," Audrey interjected. "That was so hard. What was it? Maybe a month after Marie and Eve left for New York. It took all the courage I had to get on that bus for DC, but I had a dream and we knew it was best for you and me to separate. Remember, I left you the car?"

"Oh my God, that car?" I smile at the memory of Marie working her charms to get us that car. "Marie, I'm in need of a new car. Think you can help get me a good deal?"

"Sure thing. I might be a bit rusty under this hood, but it's still working," Marie says in her best coquettish voice.

Audrey continues. "I got a job as a secretary at the Army Corps of Engineers, that's where I first met Mike who had just begun his career as an engineer. We started dating almost immediately, and we married shortly after that. I continued working, and my office skills were good, so they moved me to a more lucrative management position. After a few years, I had earned enough to quit and go fulltime to nursing school. If I couldn't have my own babies, then I could sure as hell surround myself with them and do what I could to help them survive."

"I'll bet you were a great nurse, honey," Marie says to Audrey. "Well, I never went to college, and I'll bet there's not a one of you that's the least bit surprised. I'm on husband number three. My first husband, I met the year I arrived in New York with Eve. Eve found a job at a flower shop close to our little itsy-bitsy room we were renting in the Village, and I worked as a cocktail waitress. This elderly fella came into the club where I was working one evening, and yes, I lied about my age to get the job. He was from California and he just loved my southern accent, among other things," she said with a wink. "What can I say? He was rich, and I was desperate. He died a year later, left everything to his only son, and there I was, poor little ol' me, all alone in California, my meal ticket gone. Shortly after that, I met Paul. I really loved him, but he left me after ten years for a much younger model.

I did get a nice little divorce settlement out of that one, though. Now I'm with Owen. He's a great guy, treats me like a queen, and we have a good solid marriage. We own a personal care salon in Fresno. I didn't do too bad for myself—three husbands and only one divorce." She guffaws while slapping her leg with a well-manicured hand. "I never had children either, Audrey. In fact, Bertie, you're the only one of us with children, aren't you?" Marie asks looking for confirmation.

"Yes, I guess I am," I say, acknowledging the question with surprise. "I have a daughter, Annie. She was only four when my husband Joe died. She's my world. She's also a lawyer and works with me at the firm. In fact, she gave me quite the surprise last week." I pause. "I'm going to be a grandmother!" I say with genuine excitement.

"Well, I think that calls for a celebration," Audrey says, trying to sound as enthusiastic as she can.

We spend the next hour catching up and drinking wine. Mike periodically pops in to ask about refilling our glasses and check on Audrey. He even pours her a drop at her request. "Why not? It can't hurt," she concedes.

The time flies by, but it becomes apparent that Audrey's wearing out. I don't want to leave her, and I know Audrey senses how we're all feeling.

"You know, I love you ladies. I really do." Her eyes begin to tear up. "I can't begin to tell you what seeing all of you has meant to me. Thank you for making the trip and thank you for being my friends. Now," she says, wiping her eyes with a tissue, "I know you've all got places to be, and I need a nap, but this has been the best couple of hours I've had in a long time."

Marie leans over and gives Audrey a bear hug. "Girl, we love you."

Next, Eve kneels next to Audrey, reaches up, and gently cups Audrey's thin face. "I'm so glad you asked us to come. You are so strong, and I'm lucky to have you as a friend as well."

I scoot close and take my friend's hand. "Audrey, since the day I said goodbye to you, I've felt a tremendous sadness, a real void in my life, but today I'm the luckiest person in the world for having found you again. I'm not hiding anymore. I'm here for you today and always."

"And me," Marie says.

"Count me in," replies Eve.

"You ladies are the best," says Audrey. "I want you to go live the rest of your lives, have fun, love hard, embrace all of it. Would you do that for me?"

We all assure her we will. Audrey's exhausted and lays back on the couch.

As if Mike senses his wife's fatigue, he enters and takes a seat on the arm of the sofa, next to Audrey. "Well, from the sounds of it, I'd say you ladies have been just what the doctor ordered."

Audrey reaches out and gently places her hand on his forearm, a simple gesture between a husband and wife that says so much. I don't want to leave her, but I know it's time for us to go. Audrey's tired.

I promise I'll call, as do Marie and Eve, and we each give her a final kiss. Mike assures Audrey he'll be right back and walks us to the door.

"Thank you, thank you all for coming. It's been a long time since I've heard her laugh like that and that's a gift we both will cherish." He looks intensely at each one of us, his eyes conveying the total adoration he has for his wife. I'm thunderstruck by the power of his love for her and I'm unable to speak.

Mike says goodbye, wishing us all safe travels home before turning to take care of his soulmate. The three of us linger in the driveway, not sure what comes next. These few hours together have solidified that devotion we pledged to each other all those years ago, and it's renewed our strength to move forward. Earlier today, we promised each other one more thing. Though confident that this chapter of our lives is over, we promised that if we're ever questioned by authorities in the future, we will tell the same story, the story provided to us by none other than Glennis Campbell.

"So, Eve," Marie begins playfully, "I've always been curious. Did your mother ever say whether that boy ever called your house lookin' for ya? You know that fella you got so friendly with at the Richmond bar? What was his name again?"

"Bruce!" I blurt out recalling his name.

Eve looks at Marie, then me, almost reluctant to answer. "I never gave him the correct number. I just wasn't into him."

Pent-up sorrow and tension is finally released, as we collectively burst out in gales of aching laughter, wiping tears from our eyes. I can hardly catch my breath as I recover from my hysterics. When the moment passes, and the quiet falls, my eyes linger on their beautiful faces and I say, "I guess it's time for us to go."

We don't make plans to go have drinks or meet later for dinner. Without saying it, we know it's best to say goodbye for now. We make the same promise to each other that we've made to Audrey. We will stay in touch. I'm delightfully exhausted as I start the car, but I hesitate before I pull out of the neighborhood. An idea comes to me, so instead of heading back to the hotel, I use my phone to locate a place where I can put some real closure on the day. Plus, it would be nice to spend a little time soaking up this glorious weather before returning to the hotel and preparing for my early trip home.

After a few quick searches, I locate what I hope might be a perfect spot and plug it into my GPS, heading in the direction of Alexandria. By the time I arrive, temperatures are still hovering in the seventies, the sky completely void of clouds, and brilliant sunlight bathes the day. I make my way to Founders Park, a picturesque waterfront area where I can momentarily bask in what's left of an extraordinary afternoon. I park the car, but I don't get out right away. I sit for a moment, contemplating. I know what I'm going to do, so I reach into the glove compartment and retrieve my past. Before I left the house yesterday morning, on impulse, I decided to bring the tin with me at the last minute, tucking it into the corner of my carry-on. I'm not sure why I brought it along, but I somehow felt compelled to do so. I tuck it under my arm and exit the car, clenching it tightly as I walk toward the water, following the park trail to the shoreline. A few joggers are out, and several people are walking at a leisurely pace, obviously taking advantage of the weather, too. The wind is picking up as I inch my way to the water, and though the day is relatively warm, the forceful breezes off the Potomac make me shudder, and I involuntarily wrap my arms around my chest, shielding myself from the winds. I continue walking until I come to a pier housing a couple of boats tied to their slips. I smile when I read the name of one boat, *The Escape*, painted in large gold letters on its side.

The music of the river is peaceful. I can hear the gentle slaps of waves against the creaking pier as it sways, watching and listening to the seagulls as they glide and squeal, air-cruising above the shoreline. I close my eyes and breathe in the familiar smells of my past. Though it's not the Kentucky River, it's a worthy substitute to receive the gifts I'm about to present, the bittersweet mementos of another life. I walk to the end of the pier, feeling its movement under my feet. I remove the top of the box, and extract only one picture, sliding "us" into my jacket pocket. I remove the next item, the perfume bottle, and just for a brief second, think about another bottle of perfume I was given by Marie, before heaving this one, Mama's bottle, watching it enter the water, making a rather underwhelming splash.

Next up, the bandana. I fling it, but it gets caught in suspension, before slowly hitching a ride along the river's highway. Next, the remaining photographs. For the last time, I focus on the faces of Glennis and Jesse Campbell, before tearing them both into tiny bits and releasing them like confetti. And lastly, I pick up the glass jar and hold it up to the sun, as if I'm about to make a toast. I unscrew the top and turn the bottle upside down, freeing the insect from years of incarceration. I fasten the top on the jar and place it back in the tin, before tossing them both into the Potomac. I watch it bob as the river carries away Mama's tiny green boat. I stand perfectly still until it floats away and fades from my line of sight. I'm almost done, but not quite. I look up to the afternoon sky and ask the question to the entity in charge. "Will you please forgive me for the secret I have kept?"

1975

TWENTY-THREE

Estill County, Kentucky

I t's most definitely a splash I hear. I stand as still as I can, anticipating something more to come. My need to know if Eddy's still on the bank of the river outweighs my common sense and pushes me forward. It's a stupid risk, I know, but I just gotta see if he's still there. I turn off the flashlight and stand in place long enough for my eyes to adjust to the only source of light available to me, the moon. Slowly I move toward the outline of the surrounding line of brush, staying close to the border of overgrown vegetation that leads to the river's edge. I could have sworn I heard a voice before the splash but it's probably my inner voice telling me to get the hell out of here. If Eddy's come to, I'm dead. I will myself to move forward until I see the riverbank. I can't breathe because the image I now see confirms I'm not alone. Standing in the spot where we left Eddy lying still on the bank is the silhouette of a man. It's not Eddy. This person's build is nothing like Eddy's. The man standing on the river is extremely tall and lanky like, well, like, like.... *No, no, it can't be...* He turns his head and looks in my direction. I gasp. Standing there on the river's edge is Billy. My brain tries desperately to absorb what I'm seeing, to make sense of what his being here means and where Eddy is now. It finally registers. I make the connection. I cast my wide eyes to the river, but it's impossible to make out much of anything, except the slow rush of water making its way downstream. Billy continues looking in my direction for several seconds but doesn't say a thing. I don't think he sees me, but I say nothing, waiting breathlessly for him to call out, say my name—something, anything, but he doesn't utter a single word. He simply turns and begins walking the opposite direction, following the bank of the flowing Kentucky toward town. I want to call out to him, but I'm unable to speak for fear of shattering the silence and forever changing our lives. I love him, and I understand what is happening. He's protecting me, and I'm protecting him. My heart is bleeding, and I can't stop the pain I'm feeling. Life has drastically changed. I wait until he fades out of view, then quietly make my way down to the river, casting my flashlight over the rushing water. The smell of river stew is heavy on this hot July night, and I wince from its pungent stench. I narrow my eyes, trying to zero in on anything moving in the water, but there's nothing but the force of the night's current pushing the water along. I know, deep down inside I know where Eddy is. Standing with my feet planted on the river rocks, I let the river's fingers creep close as I look for signs of him in the murky waters. I wait a full minute, shaking, watching, and listening. I hear the hum of night sounds, a melodic tune that almost lulls me into thinking all is well. Though I know it is not. I eventually turn and make my way back to the car, stopping one last time around our campsite for any items left behind. I even check the outside perimeter of the shack and its interior. Nothing that I can see is left, but it would be easy to miss something in the dark, that's for sure. I pray we haven't left anything behind, but I can't waste any more time, and my nerves are shot, so I hold tight to the radio and keep going. When I find the footpath, I turn off the flashlight as to not draw any attention. I glance behind me one more time before I leave the area and catch a flicker of something out of the corner of my eye. On the other side of the clearing I'm witnessing the faintest of nature's twinkling lightshow, and I think of Mama. Then, just for a brief moment, I let my eyes focus on the moon and I think of him and whisper, "I love you, Billy." Exhaustion has set in as I make my way up the path and back to the car. They're probably worried about me by now.

Present Day

EPILOGUE

The warm June breeze blows our hair as we come together to say goodbye to our friend. Audrey would have loved this weather; I just know it. Marie, Eve, and I stand together, paying tribute to a life well lived. I watch Mike as he tries desperately to keep his composure, but he's cried through much of the service and still his tears remain. Many of the mourners here today are the parents and their children whose lives Audrey helped save, the preemies and sick infants she nursed who are now healthy, happy children. I listen as the Lord's Prayer is recited and hold tight to Marie and Eve. I think about Annie and the grandchild I will soon have—it's a girl. I'm relieved that Annie knows the truth now. She vows to keep my story safe, not because I asked her to, but because she says I did what I had to do to survive. She's so supportive, and I'm lucky to have this daughter of mine. I think about Dolores, who's improving with each day. She won't be practicing law anymore, but she'll always be a part of our lives. Beaker even has a spring in his step. Of course, it just might have something to do

369

with the young female lawyer we've brought on board. I glance at Eve and Marie. All these people are my family. Life is precious, and I'm not wasting any more time being afraid. The service ends, we embrace, and we each say goodbye to a tearful Mike, promising we'll be here for him when and if he needs us.

I follow Eve and Marie who are walking arm in arm across the rolling green grounds of the cemetery. Though I'm full of sorrow for the loss of my friend, I smile looking at these two walking in front of me and I marvel at this unlikely pair to ever be best friends. This world will always have its share of surprises.

Marie and Eve must sense I'm focusing on them, because they simultaneously glance back, break their chain, and reach out for me to join them.

"You know, Eve, I've been thinking," Marie says. "Well, since you're a writer and all, have you ever thought about maybe writing a book about all this? You can't make this stuff up," she says with a radiant smile that's all Marie. She's goading Eve, but Eve's use to it.

"What is it they say, truth is stranger than fiction?" I add.

"Who knows, maybe I will write our story someday," Eve says. "Or maybe I've already written it." She smiles mischievously.

"Could you maybe wait and have it released, say, in about fifty years or so?" I ask with a laugh.

"Yes, I believe I can do that," she says, pulling us in tighter.

"So, what would you title it, Eve?" I ask out of genuine curiosity.

Marie doesn't wait for Eve's response but offers her own. "Oh, that's easy!" Marie exclaims. "She'd have to call it *The Fireflies of Estill County*."

The End

ABOUT THE AUTHOR

Kim E. Wilson is a graduate of the University of Louisville with a bachelor's degree in Elementary Education and a Master's in Exceptional Child Education. This is her second novel to date, with *Bird* (2019) being her first. She's a wife, a mother, and a grandmother who adores her family and resides in Louisville, KY.

Made in the USA
Columbia, SC
08 September 2020

19973339R00209